Kindred

Kindred

Tammar Stein

Alfred A. Knopf

New York

Text copyright © 2011 by Tammar Stein
Jacket art copyright © by Kamil Vojnar

All rights reserved. Published in the United States by Alfred A. Knopf, an imprint of
Random House Children's Books, a division of Random House, Inc., New York.

Knopf, Borzoi Books, and the colophon are registered trademarks of Random House, Inc.

Visit us on the Web! www.randomhouse.com/teens

Educators and librarians, for a variety of teaching tools, visit us at
www.randomhouse.com/teachers

Library of Congress Cataloging-in-Publication Data
Stein, Tammar.
Kindred / by Tammar Stein. — 1st ed.
p. cm.
Summary: Spiritual warfare breaks out when the Archangel Raphael and the Devil
deliver assignments to eighteen-year-old fraternal twins Miriam and Moses.
ISBN 978-0-375-85871-0 (trade) — ISBN 978-0-375-95871-7 (lib. bdg.)
— ISBN 978-0-375-89625-5 (ebook)
[1. Spiritual warfare—Fiction. 2. Good and evil—Fiction. 3. Supernatural—Fiction.
4. Angels—Fiction. 5. Brothers and sisters—Fiction. 6. Twins—Fiction.] I. Title.
PZ7.S821645Ki 2011
[Fic]—dc22
2010007071

The text of this book is set in 11.5-point Goudy.

Printed in the United States of America
February 2011
10 9 8 7 6 5 4 3 2 1

First Edition

To my own miracles

I.

THE FIRST TIME I MEET AN ANGEL, it is Raphael and I am eighteen.

I am not a religious girl. I do not belong to a Bible study group, though I was invited. Twice. I do not belong to a synagogue at school. Or a church, for that matter. When pressed, I admit a reluctant belief in a higher power. Reluctant, because such admissions invariably open me up to long, intense discussions. The asker wants to know either how I could possibly hold such childish and naïve beliefs, given the state of the world, or, conversely, given my said beliefs, how I could not be attending services, deepening my understanding and devotion of said higher power.

I am as comfortable speaking about my faith as I am about my sex life. That is to say, not very.

The day I meet Raphael is not a good one, though not so horrible as to merit celestial intervention. It is spring break, and I am the only student staying in the dorms on my floor. There are only three of us in the entire building. We chat a bit when we bump into each other in the common room, but the two of them are working on a project for their astronomy class. They are filled with that low-key intensity that comes from having uninterrupted time to work on an extensive project. Whereas I am here, bored and lonely, by default because my spring break plans fell through. This is my brother's fault. But more on that later.

I have never stayed in a nearly vacant building before. There are the creaks, pops and groans of an aging dormitory resting for a moment. Other than that, it is so quiet I can hear dust mites landing.

In my room, I am obeying the rules of cohabitation even though my roommate isn't here. Instinctively I find myself staying in my half of the room. Slouched on my bed, listlessly flipping through my con law textbook, I'm keeping an eye on the clock. The cafeteria has reduced hours, and though I've never cared for their food, the new, shorter mealtimes are the only thing giving my aimless days some structure. Dinner is from five to seven. Miss that and I'm stuck snacking on stale crackers or spending too much money on greasy pizza or hamburgers from the no-name restaurants nearby.

I keep an eye on the clock.

At this moment in time, if asked what I think about life, I would say that it is sometimes hard, sometimes beautiful, that we are alone in the universe, and that although there is probably a God, He is far away and not paying much attention.

I am skimming halfheartedly through the chapter on search and seizure when a tsunamic shrieking noise splits apart my dorm wall. I fall off the bed, smacking the sharp point of my elbow on the side of my desk, knocking over a chair. A cold, burning, glowing light singes my clothes, scorches my skin. The light fills the room, pouring in from the broken wall. I can't see. My bed, the desk, the chair, have disappeared in the flare. The icy light is glacier blue, exosphere thin. A voice coming from the light speaks in Ancient Hebrew. No, it *is* the light. I feel the words, the voice, reverberating down the vertebrae of my spine, coursing with the blood cells in my veins, and a terrible face neither female nor male imprints itself on the retinas behind my tightly closed eyes.

I curl into a protective comma, arms covering my head. The light tears me, burns me. I claw at my hair, my eyes, weeping. I wet myself. I pass out.

When I come to, I am sprawled on the floor in a parody of drunken abandon. I slowly sit up, drawing my limbs inward from their starfish-like stretch. Rubbing the growing bruise on my elbow and wincing from my aching head, I hold myself, crossing my arms over my chest, rocking back and forth. I notice with slight detachment that I am shaking like a struck tuning fork, vibrating.

Hesitantly, I look at the wall. It is whole, smooth, seamless. Its painted Sheetrock, scarred and dinged from years of freshman abuse, mocks the notion that anything has ever come through it. It has never split in two. Never has, never will.

There is no trace of the event. Nothing to show that I have just lost my mind except for the puddle at my feet, the deep scratches on my face.

II.

PERHAPS IT IS DIVINE INTERVENTION that made Raphael choose spring break to come visit. I spend the next three days stupefied. I can't shake the memory of that voice; the terrifying feeling of my skin scorched with ice; the wall ripped open, then closed without a seam. I look up "delusions of grandeur" on the Internet; also "schizophrenia." I read that the insane do not think they are mad. The voices in their head, they claim, come from God.

It takes three days before my subconscious gets around to translating the angel's words. I studied Hebrew for my bat mitzvah, but it's been a while.

"I am Raphael, the archangel. Evacuate Tabitha, daughter of John, before the Sabbath."

A quick search of "Raphael" and I discover that he is considered the left hand of God. The founder of medicine. The root of his name, *rapha*, is the same as the root for "medicine" in Hebrew, *rephuah*. Raphael, while giving the doctors the desire to heal, also supports the coldness needed to inflict necessary acts of pain. I decide, then and there, that I will not study medicine.

To prove to myself that it is absurd, an LSD flashback without the LSD, I ask the few remaining stragglers around campus if they know anyone named Tabitha. A last name would help, but maybe hallucinations aren't supposed to be easy.

By lunchtime, I have found the girl. It feels good to know I might not be crazy. It feels terrible to know I might not be crazy.

Tabitha is plump, with rosy cheeks and round gray eyes that twinkle with good humor. She looks like a nanny. A friendly, pretty one.

"Tabitha?" I ask.

"Hi," she says.

"I'm Miriam. Can I join you for lunch?"

She smiles and says "Sure" with such easiness, you'd think strangers joined her for lunch all the time. Maybe they do. It's odd to me, this friendliness. I haven't adjusted to college yet.

Instead, she says, "Is your last name Abbot-Levy?"

"Yeah, how'd you know?" Did Raphael speak with her too? Was she tasked with finding me and—

"Didn't you write that article about Dean Snyder's dog?" She takes a bite from her grilled cheese sandwich.

"Yeah." I smile, delighted, relieved. I am still hoping I've been hallucinating. "You're the first person who actually read my byline."

"I thought that might be you; Miriam's kind of an unusual name."

"My brother's name is Moses. So as much as I hate my name sometimes, I always remind myself it could have been worse."

She laughs.

"Miriam is a nice name," she says. "And I loved your article." I feel a warm glow at the praise. I've been writing for the school paper for three months. Interviewing people, scrambling to write down their quotes, putting it all together and then seeing my article in the paper has been the highlight of my college experience so far. More than anything else here, writing for the school paper feels like a glimpse into something I just might enjoy doing in the "real world."

Mo didn't think I'd enjoy writing for the paper. He said I was too quiet, that I wasn't nosy enough. But I've discovered you don't have to be nosy to be a good reporter. You have to be a good listener. And that I am.

"It was so sweet how Gracie would come get her when the baby cried," Tabitha says. "And then, when she had to put Gracie down and the vet kept giving dose after dose because even though she was dying, her heart was so strong . . . it was so sad." Her eyes shimmer with unshed tears, and I am amazed that my words have touched her so deeply.

"Dean Snyder comes across so tough and mean in class," I say as Tabitha sniffs a bit. "It was amazing to see this other side of her." I take a long pull from the straw in my iced tea.

The dean cried when she told me how she held Gracie long after her strong heart had finally stopped. But I didn't put that in the article.

"You took her anthro class?" Tabitha asks.

"Yeah, did you?"

"She's the toughest prof I've had. I've never worked so hard for a class."

I nod in agreement. "It's definitely one of those things you're happy you did in retrospect. At the time, it was pretty miserable."

Tabitha finishes her sandwich and I'm long done with my cup of soup, but she's easy to talk to and I'm in no hurry to leave.

I find myself telling her about my parents, the divorce, the whole twin dilemma. She's a good listener, so sincerely caring about my problems that I feel surely we were sisters in a past life. Though after a visit from an angel, maybe I shouldn't be flippant about the afterlife. I force myself to ignore that distracting thought and focus back on Tabitha. She's majoring in American archeology, which seems like it should be a summer course and not a major until she tells me about the dig she worked on in high school and how much there really is in America that is still undiscovered.

By the time lunch ends, I've confirmed that her dad's name is John and found out she lives at Parker Hall, a freshman dorm down the street from mine. We exchange phone numbers, but I haven't worked up the nerve to tell her to "evacuate," whatever the heck that means. I can't decide if I really believe. Angels do not come down from heaven and tell people what to do. As much as I like to see myself as a special, important person, there are limits to my hubris. If God was going to pick someone to contact at this school, it would be the class president or maybe that twelve-year-old genius getting his doctorate in physics, or if it was going to be a physically stressful assignment, then He'd at least pick a member of the varsity crew team.

I return to my quiet dorm to think things through. My "vision" has led me to one of the nicest people I'd ever met. Coincidence? If there is any chance my hallucination was real, shouldn't I risk looking like a lunatic and tell her to sleep at my dorm tonight? It's Friday afternoon. Assuming the messenger went by the Jewish calendar, which is what I'm going on, considering he spoke Hebrew, it will be the Sabbath in a few hours.

With my conscience pulling me, urging me on, I try calling her after lunch, but can't get through. By four I am growing nervous. Raphael, along with neglecting to give me Tabitha's last name, also neglected to give me a specific timeline. If "evacuate" meant to remove her from her dorm room, does that mean something bad is going to happen? The more time I spend alone in my room, the more I decide it does.

By six I am frantic. According to Jewish law, the Sabbath starts at sundown. Tonight, this means 6:57; I checked. I realize I have made a huge mistake. I'm an idiot. I should have said something at lunch, invited her to go to dinner, see a movie—anything to keep her away from her room. With a growing sense of urgency driving me, I call the student directory and ask for her room number.

I grab my coat and rush out into the darkening evening.

The evening is oddly warm and oppressive. I unbutton my coat, but still feel sweat bead on my upper lip and slide down my back. The campus is eerily quiet, and not nearly as bright as it should be. I hurry along the abandoned sidewalks, my footsteps echoing. None of the streetlights are lit. Nor are there lights in any of the dorm windows. Most students have left for spring break, but I can't imagine that even our penny-pinching board of visitors would turn off the streetlights to save money. I break into a run.

When I arrive at Tabitha's red-brick dorm, the sense of impending doom is so strong that I am initially relieved to find the building still standing. I half expect a *Twilight Zone*–like vanishing. There is no sign of life other than the sudden gusts of wind that grab at my coat, flapping it like awkward wings. The oak tree near Tabitha's dorm groans as the wind bends it, while brand-new spring leaves are ripped off their branches. All the hairs on my arms and the back of my neck rise, as if a giant beast were watching me. I smell ozone, and the air pressure drops so quickly my ears pop.

Too scared to turn around and see what's behind me, I bang on the front door of the building. It is always locked for safety reasons. My swipe card can only open my dorm, no one else's.

There is a loud crack from a nearby lightning strike. I bruise my fists pounding on the thick wooden door.

Suddenly it occurs to me that the locks are electronic and the power is out. I try the door and it opens so quickly that I stumble inside. I race up the stairs, panting in my heavy coat, hardly able to catch my breath in the thin air.

Tabitha lives on the third floor, and once I reach it,

I sprint down the darkened hall, pausing every few seconds to squint at room numbers. I find hers and open the door without bothering to knock.

"Tabitha," I gasp. "Run!"

She is kneeling on her bed, face pressed against the window.

"Miriam! Hi," she says, friendly and sweet as ever. "You have got to see this incredible lightning storm. I've never seen anything like it."

"Tabitha, we have to get out of here."

"It's dangerous to go out when there's lightning like this," she says, frowning. "We're safer inside. Come sit with me."

I am a woman possessed. I grab her arm, squeezing so hard it must bruise her. She instinctively pulls away. I tug her out of the door and down the hall, babbling as I go.

"Please, please come with me. I know it sounds crazy. But you have to come. I've had a—a premonition."

She lets herself be dragged along but doesn't seem to catch my panic.

"Miriam, it's okay. You're safe inside."

"No, we're not. You're not," I say, my hair sticking to my sweaty face. "I should have told you at lunch. I'm an idiot."

We make it to the stairway, and either because she believes me or to humor me, she walks with me, descending the dark staircase but not exactly hurrying.

"When did you get this"—she pauses—"premonition?" She sounds skeptical.

"A few days ago."

Which was plenty of time to get to know her and keep her out of the dorm room instead of making this panicky rescue. I want to weep in shame. Why had I waited? The danger feels very real; my doubts have vanished.

We are on the ground floor, the door still open from when I raced inside. The wind is whipping the leaves outside into small, intense whirlwinds, and the rain has started coming down in great glooping plops.

"Miriam, we shouldn't go outside with the storm coming," Tabitha says, her voice calm and kind. "We can wait in the foyer until the worst passes, and then I'll walk you to your dorm. Or you can stay with me," she offers, seeing my mulish expression.

With a growing sense of doom, I suddenly know what's going to happen.

"Is there anyone else staying at the dorm over spring break?" I ask sharply. My random question and my frightened voice take her aback.

"Um, I guess so," she says. "Probably."

Again I feel the hair on my arms rise, but this time it's pure fear. I don't waste any more words. I grab Tabitha around the waist, ignore her squeak of surprise and heft her up over my shoulder, rushing out of the building like a linebacker. I have a quick second to bless my biweekly weight-lifting sessions and the welcome, needed strength of an adrenaline rush before we are out of the building and in the shocking-cold pouring rain. I get us about fifty feet away, staggering against her struggling weight, when there is a horrendous, ground-shaking crash that throws me off my wobbling feet, sending both of us to the ground.

Tabitha lands on top of me, knocking the wind out of me before rolling to the side. I can't breathe, and for a few awful moments the world goes quiet. There is no sound. I can't hear the wind, the cars on the highway near the campus, Tabitha's shrieks or even my own heartbeat. And then, in a whoosh, all the sounds come back and I realize Tabitha isn't shrieking anymore.

The building we've just run out of has exploded. Bricks, shingles and other debris rain down around us. Curling into a tight ball, I cover my head with my arms and have a split second to think that this is the second time this week I've had to do that.

Several more explosions rock the building, and I cower, shaking, crying and praying to live through this. The solid thunking sounds of chunks of the building landing next to us echo like artillery. I glance at Tabitha curled next to me and realize there is blood pouring down her face. I scramble over to her and find her unconscious.

"No, no, no," I pant with each breath. "Don't die. Please, please. Don't." Another incredible boom and I sprawl over her as a second barrage of rubble lands all around us. The rain pours down so thickly it is nearly white. Despite that, I feel the heat coming off the building. Risking a quick glimpse up, I see it is engulfed in flames.

Within minutes, I hear a wail of sirens over the fire's roar. I ease off Tabitha and touch her face. The rain mixes with her blood to form a red froth, and I cry because there is so much of it.

The flashing red and white lights of the emergency vehicles join the blue lights of police cars, the yellow of the fire and the dull gray of the rain.

"Ma'am, ma'am . . ." A voice bursts through my grief. "Are you all right?"

It is the dumbest question I have ever heard.

"She's hurt," I say. "Help her."

Another person, barely recognizable as human under all the reflective fire-retardant gear, kneels by us, and the two of them begin stanching Tabitha's wounds and assessing her for injuries. A third man wraps a thin silver blanket around my shoulders and forces me away from her.

"There's still a danger of more explosions!" he shouts in my ear over the sirens of still-arriving emergency vehicles and the surprisingly loud sounds of the building burning behind us. "You must step away. They'll take care of your friend."

I let him lead me because I know there isn't anything else I can do to help Tabitha. I had my chance.

They take me to the ER, but other than treating me for shock with orange juice and oxygen, and for a strained shoulder with an ice pack, I'm fine. I am barely scratched. I slip away when the nurse isn't looking.

Tabitha isn't as lucky. Aside from a concussion, she has a bone-deep gash that needs twenty stitches, and an orbital fracture that causes her right eye to droop lower than her left. This will affect her vision and is probably permanent, I hear the doctor say. She can't remember much. She doesn't know how she ended up outside her building. She doesn't recall ever meeting me.

The two other students in the dorm building that night died. The local paper publishes long, extravagant obituaries, but the next day, I make inquiries of my own. They'd been involved in a fraternity hazing that killed a freshman the semester before. One of them had killed a mother of three in a drunk-driving accident during high school. His parents paid handsomely, and a lawyer got him off. The other had had two different rape charges brought against him and later dismissed. My mind shies away from thinking that they deserved to die. That the left hand of God killed them.

I go to the library and read about Sodom and Gomorrah. The angels say to Lot: "Take them out of this place, for we are about to destroy it, because the outcry is so great before the Lord that He has sent us to destroy it." My face grows hot and cold, spots dance before my eyes. I keep reading. "In the morning, Abraham went to the place where he had stood before the Lord. And he looked out toward Sodom and Gomorrah, and toward all the region of the Plain, and saw the smoke from the land rising like the smoke of a furnace." I run to the bathroom and throw up.

I want to speak with Tabitha, but each time I draw near, I can't bring myself to walk up to her, to introduce myself again. The accident has changed her. Instead of the open, friendly look she used to have, as if someone had just told her some pleasant news, she now keeps her head down, her shoulders hunched up defensively. She was supposed to have been spared. It is all my fault.

III.

IN THE FIFTEENTH CENTURY, a young peasant girl in rural France experienced a series of encounters with heavenly voices. They came first as a bright light, but over time coalesced into perfect, beautiful visions. The archangel Michael was there, along with several other saints the girl recognized. These visions were so lovely that she cried when they ended. The angel and the saints told her that she must help recover her homeland, devastated from decades of war and pillage.

She was young when these visions began, only thirteen. They continued for years. Years of visions telling her she must overcome her fears, her reluctance, her previous understanding of her place in the world. Until finally, at age seventeen, she no longer doubted.

She petitioned the local garrison commander to visit the

royal French court. Once there, she convinced the prince to let her lead his army against the British, who were holding the city of Orléans under siege. This siege had been dragging on for months when she arrived, a young medieval woman completely unversed in military strategy or tactics.

Within ten days, she ended it. This was the start of her military career. Over the course of the next eighteen months, she was severely injured several times, ignored by seasoned generals and adored by the army and the people of France.

During one retreat, she was among the last to leave the field and was captured and held for ransom. Her peasant family could not pay, and the prince, fearing her growing popularity, would not step in to help. She was sold to the British.

This story does not end well.

The girl goes on trial for heresy. Her crime was not hearing voices, but rather the sin of wearing men's clothing. No one seems to have doubted her claim that God's emissaries spoke to her; they were only looking for a loophole to stop her. The bishop leading the trial did not follow the laws and conventions of the ecclesiastical court. Some of the clergy on the tribunal had been coerced to serve. The girl's answers were eloquent and correct, yet she was found guilty and burned at the stake. Concerned that her remains would be a rallying point or, worse, become holy relics, the men who had burned her insisted that her charred body be burned twice more and her ashes scattered on the Seine. The executioner later said he feared he was damned for doing such a thing.

The girl's name was Joan of Arc. And even though she did

everything she was supposed to do, everything God wanted her to do, by the time she was nineteen, she was dead.

Never mind the fact that a mere twenty-four years later, the pope exonerated her and removed the stigma of heresy. Never mind that in 1920 she was named a saint. It's pretty obvious that though her short life was full of glory, it was also full of agony, injustice, cruelty and, ultimately, betrayal.

I have always known the basics of Joan's story, but it is as if I am learning it for the first time. It sickens me, the gross injustice of it all. The unfairness not just of those wicked, evil men, but of the messengers from God who started it, who set her on her path.

Where were they?

It's clear flipping through history books and reading about the people who claim angels appeared before them (outside of the patriarchs of the Bible, and not counting poor Joan) that they aren't exactly a who's who of sanity or importance. Besides having a disturbing tendency to be burned at the stake—don't think for a moment Joan was the only one—most of them were also a bunch of raving, uneducated, borderline insane, sad, pathetic losers. And now I have joined their ranks. Except I have none of Joan's courage, her great wit, or her convictions, and I have already failed at the one task set before me.

Joan was left to suffer a brutal execution after fulfilling all her duties. God only knows what's going to happen to me.

After spring break ends and students fill the classrooms, dorms and cafeteria, nothing is the same. Tabitha's photo is on the front page of the school paper, with the screaming headline

FREAK ACCIDENT KILLS TWO, DISFIGURES HONORS STUDENT. I haven't been there since before the accident, but I should have realized the paper would cover the story and tried to blunt its insensitivity toward Tabitha. I grab all the copies I can find and dump them in the recycling bin, but I know I can't recycle every one on campus. For once, I'm not proud to be part of the paper. The article isn't well written or kind; it's simply juicy. National media have picked up the story, too, and for a couple of days, large vans with boil-like transmitters growing from their roofs dot the campus. Several students and administrators are blasted with bright lights as they try to sound intelligent in front of the cameras, answering a barrage of mostly trivial questions. The university president assures the public that there will be an investigation as to why the dormitory didn't have a lightning rod as per state safety regulations and why the chemistry department was storing large containers of acetone, hydrogen peroxide and sulfuric acid · in the attic. Everyone agrees that it would have been an unimaginable tragedy if the freak storm had occurred a mere week earlier or later. Hundreds of students would have been killed.

I overhear someone say, "Thank God it happened when it did."

Students flip through the paper in the cafeteria, out on the quad and in halls between classes. Tabitha's pain and suffering are put on public display. Every grimace, every sigh of pity, is like a stabbing finger pointing out my shame, her pain, everywhere I turn.

Damn paparazzi, I think. Then I clap my hands over my

mouth, because isn't damning someone the same as taking the Lord's name in vain?

I drift through classes, hardly hearing my professors, hardly caring about the lectures, not bothering to take notes or read the assigned chapters. I expect another visit at any minute. I look for signs from God in every wind gust, every bird that flutters up from the ground, startled by my passing. I develop odd cramps and unexplained bouts of diarrhea that come and go and have me running to the bathroom at the most inconvenient moments.

Two weeks after spring break, I start skipping classes altogether, spending my time deep in the bowels of the library, reading everything I can on angels, on celestial contact with humans, on miracles. There isn't much. What there is, as with the example of Joan of Arc, isn't very promising. Web sites are even worse. Frightening, delusional blogs; inaccurate retellings of historical incidents; cheesy graphics that mock my terror.

I have failed Tabitha. I have let down God Himself in high heaven. I don't know where to take my shame, whom to turn to for comfort.

I'm not sure how long I would have continued to float in this purgatory, waiting for a word, looking for a sign. Fortunately, Mo comes in for his long-delayed visit.

"Sis," he says after our usual big bear hug, "you look awful. What the hell have you been doing?"

Mo, my twin, is three inches taller than me. He is thin and wiry, with dark curly hair that tends to bush out if he waits too long between haircuts. We look startlingly alike, as near to identical as brother and sister can be. Looking at his face, I see what I would look like as a man.

"I've had this nasty bug. I've lost a bit of weight," I say.

He immediately takes a few steps back and makes a cross with his fingers. "And you hugged me? Jesus, Miriam, I don't want to catch the plague."

I laugh. He ducks, covering his nose and mouth so that his hands are like a gas mask.

"I don't think it's contagious, no one else seems to have it. Besides, I'm pretty much over it."

"In that case, let's get some food and put some meat on your bones. You look like death." He walks out of my dorm room and I hurry after him. He is wearing jeans and a bright green and yellow Brazilian soccer jersey. I am wearing jeans and a green-and-yellow-striped polo shirt. We did not plan to wear the same colors, but it often happens. We no longer remark on it.

"You're sweet," I coo. "You know just how to flatter a girl. Are you sure you have a girlfriend?"

"Actually, we broke up."

I put a hand on his arm. "Mo, I'm sorry." But he dances away and grins.

"Don't worry, there weren't hard feelings. It's not like I'm looking for a wife."

"I liked Amber," I say. Even though I didn't, really. She was nice enough, but a little dim. Still, she was the first person Mo actually deigned to call a girlfriend, so no matter what his devil-may-care attitude said, she was important to him.

"Who broke it off, you or her?"

"Miriam, knock it off, okay? It doesn't matter."

It must have been Amber for him to be so touchy.

He walks faster, and I break into a trot to keep up. Ever since the accident, my energy has been sapped by worry, guilt and indecision about my future. Those odd bouts of stomach cramps haven't helped. I didn't realize how out of shape I've grown during the time. My legs feel rubbery and weak.

"Slow down," I gasp. "I can't keep up."

He stops and looks at me, half irritated, half concerned.

"You're running," I complain. "You know I hate running."

"For God's sake, Miriam, you are in sorry shape if you can't walk half a mile to dinner."

I wince as he takes the Lord's name in vain. I've started noticing how often people do that, carelessly. I want to tell him, to tell them all, to be careful.

Mo opens his mouth to say something else, but stops himself. He takes a breath as if to speak, but then thinks better of it.

For the first time since the angel's visit, something other than biblical worries has caught my attention. There is something shimmering off my brother. I don't know if it is the breakup or the mysterious reason he postponed his visit, but something momentous has happened to Mo and I finally notice that he is bursting to tell me.

He looks both ways as if checking for eavesdroppers, which is ridiculous on a Tuesday evening in the middle of campus. Then he shakes his head.

"I have to tell you something, but I can't talk about it here. Let's grab a couple of burgers and head to the trails, okay?"

The "trails" are a set of paths in the park near school. During the day, they are a favorite jogging path of the more athletically inclined of the student body, the would-be marathoners and athletes. They are secluded enough that you can almost pretend you are out in the woods, away from the town and the campus and civilization. They are also the site of an occasional rape or assault, pretty much for the same reason. I never go there at night. But Mo is with me, so after a short hesitation, I shrug and say okay.

After picking up some burgers and fries, we carry our bags, with their blooming stains of grease, and hike up a narrow path of trampled-down dirt. My breath is catching again, and the smell of fries growing cold isn't appetizing. Nothing like congealing grease to ease stomach cramps.

"This is far enough," I say. My heart is beating too fast, almost painfully thudding. I press a hand to my chest. "I think I'm having a heart attack."

"You're pathetic," Mo says. But I notice with petty satisfaction that his lip is dotted with sweat even though the night is cool.

"*We're* pathetic," I correct. "Maybe we should take some sort of exercise vow."

He ignores me, and we continue grunting and puffing upward. I point out a large, flat rock near the trail, and after a quick glance around, Mo agrees we've walked far enough.

"So, what's the story?" I ask as we settle down. I make a show of unwrapping my burger but then let it sit in my lap. I feel nauseous from the smell.

"You're going to have a really hard time believing me," he

says, for once looking uncertain. "But no matter how crazy this sounds, I'm telling the truth and you have to promise not to tell anyone. Not anyone."

"Okay."

"No, Miriam." He grabs my arm near the elbow, hard enough to make me jump. "I'm serious. You can't tell anyone. I don't even know if I'm supposed to tell you, but no one said I couldn't, so . . ."

"What, Mo? What happened?"

But here's the thing. I already know.

"I met someone."

"A girl?" I know that isn't it, but it's what a normal person would assume. Right now, I'm fighting hard to be normal.

"No, not even close. Miriam, I spoke to God. Well, not exactly God, but basically, yeah, I did."

"Really?" I don't doubt him. Still, he doesn't look shaken.

"Well, mostly I listened. He told me all sorts of amazing things, incredible things. He showed me things I never would have believed. Miriam, everything we learned, it's true and not true. I mean, there is a God, there is heaven and hell and everything. But the Bible—our parents, they got it all wrong! Miriam, it was the most amazing night of my life. Everything fell into place—all the things I ever wondered about or thought about, I know. I know."

"You know what?" My own visit had only left me with questions, with doubt, with fear, while his sounded like a blessing, a benediction.

"I don't know. Everything, I guess."

"What does that mean?" I feel my cheeks flush with anger.

24

Until this moment, I had thought that although my burden was heavy, I had been blessed. Maybe I had let God down, but I was special, I was chosen. Instead, I suddenly see that I suffered through a horrible, painful ordeal, but my brother, my naughty, mischievous brother, received the key to everything. It has been many years since I felt like stomping my feet and yelling "NOT FAIR!" but I feel like it now.

"So, what's the big revelation?"

He looks at me with slight pity. "I can't tell you."

I want to smack him on the back of the head. "Excuse me?"

"Miriam, I can't. It's not something I can put into words. It's just this feeling, this wonderful feeling." He laughs. It should be joyful laughter, but there is something nasty there too.

"Anyway, I have a task to do, something really secret and important."

"Doesn't everyone," I mutter, but he doesn't hear me.

"I really can't tell you about it, but I can't get over that I was picked. I was chosen!" He whoops with sudden glee and hugs me roughly. I can't help but catch his excitement. He is my brother. I hug him back, tightly.

"Don't slack off," I warn. "You'd better get this done, whatever it is. You wouldn't have been asked if it wasn't important." I don't know why I don't tell him about my own experience. Maybe I am ashamed that mine was so awful, while his was glorious. Maybe I can't bring myself to admit that I have failed God, while he seems set to succeed. I have always been the steady one, the reliable one. I want to tell him that, but I don't.

25

"God, you think I don't know that?" I wince at his curse. "As soon as I get back from visiting you, I'm on it. I have a plan."

"Good," I say. "That's good. Are you sure you should be taking the Lord's name in vain?"

"Chill, okay? Believe me when I tell you the Big Man is above such things. He doesn't care what you call anything."

The night has grown chilly, and I hug my light cotton sweater around me.

Mo says he's leaving tonight, driving four hours back to his university even though he'd just arrived this afternoon. An eight-hour drive for a three-hour visit. But I don't try to talk him into staying. I know the cost of procrastination where divine missions are involved.

As we make our way down the path in the rapidly fading light, I realize that I can't face going back to campus. Going to my room, reading three chapters on the Constitution, writing a fifteen-page paper, preparing for a quiz—it all seems like meaningless fluff, a ridiculous waste of my time and a charade I can't go through. With Mo beside me nearly glowing with zeal and excitement, I realize that after such a colossal mistake, I can't go back.

"I have news too," I say, hearing the words come out of my mouth and knowing suddenly what I am going to do. "I'm leaving school."

"You mean you're transferring? Did you change your mind about going to Tech?"

"No," I say. "I'm dropping out." It is the first time I have thought about it, but I immediately feel better. I need to move on. I need to answer some questions.

"Holy shit, Mom and Dad are going to freak!" He does a little dance. "You know what this means?"

I shake my head.

"I'm the good one! I'm the good son and you're the prodigal daughter. Hallelujah, who thought this day would ever come?"

"Glad it made your day." I pretend to kick him and he dances out of the way. But sensing some of my despair, Mo settles down.

"Miriam, you've never done anything in your whole life without a good reason," he says. "You don't even sneeze without thinking about it first. If you've decided to drop out, then knowing you, you spent a month making lists of pros and cons. Am I right?"

How can I tell him I have literally decided to drop out this minute? "You know me," I say tightly. "Besides, I'm only eighteen. I have time before I have to settle down."

"See? I'm not worried about you. You know how to take care of yourself. Forgive me for delighting in my temporary role as the favorite—we both know it won't last long. You're probably going to write the Great American Novel and I'll be the loser brother again."

I feel a swell of love and exasperation.

"Mo, you're full of it."

We share a smile as we reach his car, a beat-up, rusty black Suburban.

27

"Be careful, okay?" I tell him. "Whatever it is you're supposed to do, it might be dangerous."

"Nah," he says as he climbs into the high cab. He starts the truck with a roar and then rolls down the window. "You take care of yourself, and remember, I've got friends in low places."

"Don't you mean high places?"

"It'll be high enough soon enough."

"Wait, what?"

The taillights flash red as he shifts into gear. "Don't tell me you haven't figured it out!" he says. "I talked to someone who has all the power and all the answers. Someone who *rewards* his followers. Who does that sound like? The one who, just for laughs, put Job through hell? I don't think so. I met the guy with the real power. He's gotten a hell of a bad rap." He snorts at his pun. "He's amazing and awesome. He's everything I ever wanted to be—charismatic, brilliant, generous. I hope you'll get to meet him one day. You'd love him."

I stare at him in slack-jawed horror.

"Tell me you're joking."

He grins. "I got to go. Call me, sis!"

Satan, Lucifer, Azazel, the devil. My twin brother has met the devil, *likes him*, and is now doing him a favor.

I lift my hand in an automatic wave, struck dumb by his words.

IV.

BACK AT THE LIBRARY, I sit alone, trying to process what
I've discovered. Twins who are approached by the far ends of
the good-evil spectrum? Yeah. I don't bother Googling, I *know*
there's nothing online about this. I chew my thumbnail as
I try to decide if I should pray for my twin's soul. But honestly,
that might only make things worse. I tell myself maybe the
rules are different for someone like Mo. Mo's real name is
Moses. Yes, my parents actually named us Miriam and Moses.
They liked that they're siblings in the Bible, and better them
than Tamar and Amnon, since Amnon rapes his half sister
Tamar and then is killed by his half brother Absalom, who is
then killed by his father's soldiers to avenge Amnon's death.
They figured any of those three might be a bit over the top.
You think? Still, Miriam and Moses? It's just wrong. When we
entered elementary school, Moses somehow turned into Mo

and the nickname stuck. It was a better fit, although pretty much any name would be. I tried to go by Miri, Mir, and M., but none of those nicknames ever caught on. Everyone kept calling me Miriam, and sometime around tenth grade I gave up.

Our parents divorced when Mo and I were eleven. At first there was talk of separating us, keeping me with Mom and Mo with Dad. Maybe alternating summers with us together with each parent. Mo put an end to that. He'd been listening in on the other phone as Mom's lawyer first suggested the possibility of a split. Mo didn't even tell me. He attacked. Vandalism, trouble at school—he pulled out every weapon in his eleven-year-old arsenal. Within a month we were all seeing a therapist, who emphatically recommended keeping us together.

"Twins," he reminded my parents, "are closer than traditional siblings. Modern science is still learning about the emotional and perhaps even mental bond between them. The trauma of separating them at this age could be"—he paused—"incalculable."

Mo looked over at me and gave me a thumbs-up.

My parents figured out a way to share custody that didn't mean splitting us. Instead of moving back to England, Mom kept her job in the theology department at the university and moved out of the city, to an old, rambling cottage in the country. Dad, also a professor of theology, bought a large apartment downtown. They saw each other at staff meetings and occasionally in the hallways of the department, but off duty, they pretty much ensured they wouldn't see each other at the grocery, bank or any other public setting.

Mo and I, attending the same school, switched months living with our mom and our dad until we left for college.

I rub my knees, half noticing that they feel achy and hot. I briefly wonder at this weird constellation of problems that has suddenly erupted. My stomach, my joints, my energy level. I'm irritated and a little scared. I've never had anything worse than a cold. I never get sick. I was so annoyed and jealous when Mo got mono and I didn't. He missed a week of ninth grade.

I shouldn't be surprised Mo is enamored with the devil. He always had a different way of seeing things. Apart from that week of mono, which he managed to parlay into getting out of a final project in our European history class, he was also our high school mascot at football games for our last two years of school—which meant he traveled with the football team to away games. He was the founder of the school's poker and investment clubs, organizing the school's first poker tournament, with the prize money, a thousand-dollar scholarship, put up by local businesses. Naturally he won, even though he didn't need the money.

No one else had his extensive social network, his connections. He was always ready for a laugh, saying anything that popped into his mind. And Mo noticed things most people missed.

The summer of our senior year, Mo and I spent a lot of time at the local pool.

"Check it out," Mo said, pointing at the sunbather near us. "It's the third time she's sprayed crap on herself."

The woman was gorgeous, with a tiny sky-blue bikini highlighting curves even I had to admit were eye-catching.

"I'm going to investigate," he said, winking at me before ambling over to her. He should have looked ridiculous—a high school boy, short for his age and wearing Hawaiian-print board shorts that hung way too long. Instead, he looked cocky and, in a way I couldn't define, like someone who knew what he wanted and liked what he saw.

Within seconds the two were chatting away, and I found myself scooting over a couple of lounge chairs so I could eavesdrop.

"It's for my job," the woman said, waving at the suntan lotion.

"Oh, you're a stripper?" Mo said.

I couldn't suppress a wide-eyed glance at the two of them. His nerve asking someone that blew me away, and I expected her to storm off in a huff, maybe slap him on her way. Instead, she was mildly surprised.

"How did you know?"

I nearly choked on my soda. Mo shot me a look.

"Who else needs a perfect tan?" he said with the world-weary ennui of a frequent strip-club patron. Two boys in identical blond haircuts and matching swim trunks hurried over, dripping and shivering slightly, to beg for ice cream money. She reached into the beach bag on the ground next to her and pulled out some crumpled bills.

"My husband's a contractor," she told Mo once the boys were out of earshot. "With the market turning the way it did, we lost so much money that we were close to bankruptcy. I stripped in college and I was still in good shape, so . . ."

"And the money's good?" asked my shameless brother.

"Look, I don't turn tricks, I don't lap-dance, I just strip and I make about twelve grand a month. In six more months we'll be completely out of debt and I'll quit."

My brother nodded thoughtfully. "I have to ask, are they real?"

"Excuse me?" Her tone grew cold.

"Your nails," he said, straight-faced.

"They're fake," she said, studying her hands. Then she paused and cracked a smile. "Both of them." This time I thought I might need the Heimlich to get a piece of ice unstuck from my throat, and my choking fit was loud enough to catch her attention. She looked over at me, then back at my brother, and smiled.

"You two look identical."

I scowled as Mo cracked a joke about his "manly" sister, but let him get away with it. I knew it bothered him when people said we looked alike. He was always small for his age, with ridiculously long eyelashes. Eventually we went back in the water, where Mo promptly dunked me and tried to pants me, yanking at my bikini bottoms. I retaliated by splashing so much that one of his contact lenses floated away.

"See," Mo said later as I drove us home. "Not all sin is bad. Sometimes it can save good people."

It was an old debate in our family. The nature of good and evil. Free will. Thoughts versus actions. Intent and consequences.

"We both know she's not quitting in six months," I said. "After they're out of debt, their car'll need repairs. And after the car is fixed, the kids'll need braces. There's always going to be something. How long before she is doing lap dances? If she earns twelve grand stripping, she'll make more turning tricks. I'm not saying she will, but she's living in a dangerous place."

"Miriam," Mo said, sighing and closing his eyes. "Shut up."

I don't know why I expected telling my parents that I'm dropping out would go well. Neither one of them screams, calls me names or makes threats. But that hurt, baffled look on my dad's face goes a long way toward curdling the chowder I had for lunch. My father simply asks me why, and I know he expects a better answer than a shrug. "College is stupid," I mumble, half ashamed. "It's a waste of time."

"What's so much better than improving your mind and preparing yourself for a career?"

Considering the shock of my announcement, it's impressive he stays so calm. He has a temper, though it has mellowed with age. The compressed lips, the tightening around his eyes . . . I brace myself, thrown back to age ten, when he could reduce me to tears with a look. He doesn't yell at me now. He looks old and tired. He looks disappointed. I think about this from his perspective, and it doesn't look good. If he would get nice and pissed, then I could be defensive. This weariness just leaves me feeling guilty.

What am I leaving college for? What better options do I see for myself? Good questions. Ones I don't have answers to. I consider telling him about my visit. But I can't find the words. Tell my father—the learned rabbi, the tenured professor—that I have been given a mission by an archangel, only to fail? There are lots of things I regret, but not telling my dad about meeting Raphael isn't one of them.

My mother cries when I tell her. Her small house in the country is the antithesis of my father's modular Swedish Modern city apartment. We sit at the kitchen table with mugs of tea.

I'm shocked when I see her eyes well with tears.

"No, Mom, don't," I say, grabbing for the hand not holding the tea. "Please don't." Answering tears well up in my own eyes.

When she sees that, she smiles, and soon both of us give a watery chuckle. I have always cried when others cry. I can't help it. She pats my hand and then grabs both of us a tissue. I blow my nose and bury my face in my mug of tea, avoiding my warped reflection.

"I'll pray for you," she says. "To help you find your way. For clarity."

"Thank you."

She doesn't ask many questions. But then, she never has. She always is receptive to talks, confessions, but she doesn't probe. After that first show of emotion, she's much calmer and doesn't seem as devastated as my father, though clearly she's confused. I don't tell her about Raphael either, though as a former nun I think she would have taken the news better than my father would have. But it doesn't seem right to tell one parent and not the other. Ever since the divorce, I try hard to be fair. To keep things balanced.

In the end, we reach an agreement. My parents won't try to stop me from this oddly destructive (from their point of view) hiatus from college. In return for this benevolence, I'm to call in once a week and report where I am and what my plans are for the upcoming week.

This is a very decent agreement, but I feel slightly sick from my deception. I never say I have a plan, but I don't dissuade them from their assumption that I must have something in mind.

After I tell my mother my big news, I call Mo. I start to talk but soon choke up.

"What's wrong?" he asks. I hear the intense concern in his voice. Until I started crying, he was probably e-mailing or watching a game. Mo tends to multitask. But now I can feel him turning away from everything except the sound of my voice. "Miriam, what's wrong?"

I want to tell him. It's like a weight in my mouth, in the back of my throat, the words choking me. "I can't tell you on the phone," I manage to say. My chin is wobbling from the effort to hold back.

"So come see me." He knows I'm at Mom's, which means I'm ninety minutes away by train. I hear rapid clicking as he checks train schedules online. "There's an Amtrak that leaves in an hour. Get your ass on it."

The train station closest to Tech is a lovely pale gray

building from the early 1900s, with all the beauty that architects seemed to invest in their work back then. Rising two and a half stories, its façade has weathered gently, radiating calm stability. Sea-green stained-glass windows glow like planets in the evening. But the area of town the station is in hasn't aged as well. An interstate overpass looms above the parking lot, so everything is in perpetual gloom and clatter, while the surrounding empty lots are enclosed in chain-link fences, as if to prevent shards of glass, crushed paper sacks and other urban flotsam from escaping. I step off the train and see Mo leaning against a pillar, waiting for me. When I see him— the crooked smile, that wiry energy—I can't hold back any longer. I run over and hug him fiercely. After a second of startled surprise, he wraps his arms around me tight.

"Hey, Miriam," he says softly, his face in my hair. "You're okay."

I finally let go, already feeling better.

We walk back to his car, and sitting there in the parking lot, the car idling, the heat on, I spill all my secrets.

Mo's dark eyes grow round with excitement, and he starts laughing. "No way, no way, that's so freakin' awesome!" I should have known my brother would have an unpredictable response. "That's what you're all upset about?" He shakes his head before letting out another howl of laughter.

"But don't you see?" I say, trying to get his attention, to break his maniacal laughter. "I failed. I. Failed."

"Miriam," he says, placing a warm hand on my shoulder. "You didn't fail. You saved the girl, while the bastard bad guys fried. That's all anyone wanted you to do. And you did it."

"You didn't see her face, Mo." My stomach still twists and cramps when I remember the pooling blood and the way Tabitha's eye drooped so low I could see the entire curve of her eyeball. "She's good. Good with a capital G. Bible good. She's kind and sweet. She wasn't supposed to be hurt."

"First of all, sis, if it was that important, then I think the Big Guy upstairs could have held off another couple of seconds to make sure you two were clear of the falling debris."

I start to say something, but he goes on.

"Second, maybe the angel shouldn't have spoken in Ancient Hebrew and in code, don't you think? What's wrong with plain English? Why make it a big mystery for you to figure out? You had a lot of hurdles to clear, and you did what you were supposed to do. You should be proud of yourself, not upset."

I appreciate the pep talk, and I really appreciate that in Mo's eyes, at least, I'm not a horrible person. But it doesn't change my basic belief that I was supposed to spare Tabitha pain and suffering and I hadn't done that.

Mo mistakes my silence for agreement.

"My task wasn't nearly as complicated," he says, by way of explanation.

I give him a funny look. "I don't know that comparing the way the devil works with God's way is a good tactic to win an argument." Mo's truck reeks of something I can't place. That and his annoying tendency to turn everything into a debate erodes any sense of relief I felt in sharing my secret.

"We aren't having an argument," he says. "I just think it's interesting. Everyone always portrays things as black-and-white, good or evil, but really, what in life is that simple? I think we, as a civilization, don't have a clear view of what the celestial breakdown is really like.

"Unlike your painful, terrifying encounter, with its confusing task, my visit was very pleasant, almost magical, where everything was revealed and my task clearly explained. He even gave me suggestions for how to do it."

"Rub it in," I grumble. "And what did you do?"

"He told me to go to the library and cut three pages out of a certain book. I did. End of story."

I wait for him to continue, but he just sits there.

"And . . . ," I prompt.

"That's it. Mission accomplished."

"No, it's not. It can't be," I say, annoyed. "You didn't think to wonder why the devil might want you to do this?"

He looks uncomfortable for a moment but recovers fast, coming right back at me.

"I'm not an idiot, Miriam," he says, glaring at me. "Of course I wondered."

We're both quiet for a second before he continues, defensively. "There was some schmuck who was expelled on honor charges. He was the last person to check out the book for a class assignment, so they figured he cut the pages so no one else could use them."

My eyes grow round.

"You got someone kicked out of school?" I ask in outrage.

"Whatever," Mo says. "He was an asshole. He deserved it."

"Oh, really. Why was he an asshole?"

"He was born that way, okay? Shit, Miriam, what the hell do you want from me?" he says, raking a hand through his hair. We sit quietly in the car, the hum of the heater the only sound. I don't look at him. "He really was a jerk," Mo says after a moment. "He even served time in juvie, okay? I checked."

"That doesn't make sense, Mo," I say quietly. "Why would the devil want someone like that kicked out?"

"Look, I don't know and I don't care. Nothing is simple in life. We can't ever know the whole story, so we do what we can to take care of ourselves." Nothing he says sits right with me. He's missing a huge point: a kid from juvie who goes to college is special, someone who's turning his life around, except he's just been dealt a huge blow and he'll probably never get another chance. But I don't know if Mo's ignoring this because he doesn't want to see it or because he's been bedazzled. My lunch, a slice of deep-dish cheese pizza from the dining car, turns uneasily in my stomach.

"How can you say that?" I ask. "My task was to *save* someone and your task was to *ruin* someone. The difference matters, Mo."

Mo, who is studying advertising, has yet another easy answer.

"Listen, sis," he says, not unkindly. "We've somehow tapped into major power. Major. The biggest power there is. You're with God, I'm with the devil." He says that like it doesn't matter which is which. Like it doesn't mean that one of us is doing evil things. "Do you realize how powerful that makes us? We could rule the world."

"Now you're scaring me." I turn away and stare blindly out the window. It's fogging up, airbrushing away that dismal parking lot, the urban decay. It still looks depressing. "I don't think you get it. We're nothing to them. Tools. Maybe even less than that. We're totally discardable, paper napkins to wipe their hands with and throw away."

"I wouldn't be so quick to say that. They need us. I'll do the first few chores gratis, but after that, my man downstairs is going to pay."

"What, like you're a crack dealer? You're going to get him hooked on you? Don't kid yourself." My brother isn't evil. I know he isn't. My twin brother, with my identical brown eyes that always seem like they are laughing, his face as familiar to me as my own. I just have to talk some sense into him. "If it's really Satan you're dealing with, he's had centuries to manipulate people—millennia. Remember that nice little couple, Adam and Eve? Didn't turn out so great for them. A semester and a half in advertising is not going to bring you on par with the Master of Deception."

I'm not getting through to him. His eyes are shining, he can't stop grinning.

"What about your soul, Mo?" I ask, feeling frightened. "Aren't you scared?"

But Mo isn't scared. Mo is excited.

I leave after Mo buys me dinner at the student cafeteria. He sneaks out a couple of apples and a roll for me to take. I have to be careful with my money. I emptied out my bank account and have to make my meager savings last until I figure out what to do with my life. But this fine line between sin and mischief, between cleverness and manipulation, haunts me. I accept the smuggled food with mixed feelings.

"Call me if you need anything," he says, hugging me fiercely. "Though I'm sure you'll be okay—I mean, you've got angels watching over you, babe."

I give him a weak smile.

"But sometimes," he continues, "you need a little devil on your side. So don't forget, I've got connections."

V.

I DON'T KNOW if Mo is right or not. Maybe angels are watching over me. Maybe a bit of his devil's luck rubs off. Either way, I do pretty well as a college dropout.

My advisor, who was rather shocked when I told him I was taking a "leave of absence," e-mails me the week after I quit school with the contact information for a small paper in Tennessee that's looking to hire a full-time assistant.

"Thought it sounded perfect for you," he writes. "It would help to keep busy and make a bit of money when you're looking for answers. I know the editor; we were in the army together. I took the liberty of sending him a couple of your pieces from the school paper. He's interested. Here's his number. Do me a favor and call."

I'm torn. On the one hand, the little money I have is disappearing faster than I ever imagined. At this rate, I'll be broke by week's end. But then again, I can't shake the feeling of a giant bull's-eye on my back. I don't sleep well at night. I'm scared to be alone. I'm leery of anything that smacks of "destiny" or "fate," afraid of where it might lead me. Am I supposed to go to this small town in Tennessee? Is this part of God's plan for me? I don't dare say no, but I'm afraid to go. I worry daily about another visit.

But finally, after sitting in a diner and ordering the cheapest thing on the menu and leaving still feeling hungry, I decide to call. It's ridiculous to think that sleeping someplace different every night will actually keep me hidden from whatever God has in mind for me.

One phone call later, I am gainfully employed by the *Hamilton Morning Gazette*. My new boss expects me to be at work the following Monday, but doesn't offer to pay for a ticket that would get me to Tennessee. Given that my salary isn't discussed either, I begin to have a fairly good idea that this isn't a job one takes for the financial benefits. Still, it's better than what I've got now, and it's nice having a bit of purpose in life again.

I call my parents to report in.

"I'll be in Tennessee, about eight hours away. I've got a job at the local paper there."

"That's great," my mom says with some relief.

"I don't know that I'll be writing articles right away, but I'll let you know when I get published." Oddly enough, dropping out of college has actually turned out to be a good career move. I'm about to write for a real, commercial paper. It's a small ray of hope that life as I know it isn't actually over.

"Okay, sweetheart, I'm glad you'll be staying put for a bit and not that far away. Are you feeling okay?"

I'd told my mom about the occasional bouts of diarrhea I've had. "It's been clearing up," I say. "It just took a while to get used to all that greasy school food. Not that I'm complaining; this has been the best weight-loss program I've ever been on."

"You don't need to lose weight," she says a bit sharply.

"I'm fine, Mom."

"I won't nag, but you need to take care of yourself. Part of being an adult is taking care of the body God gave you."

Oh, the irony.

"I've got to go," I say.

"Safe travels, my love," she says. "Call me when you get to Tennessee? I know it's not part of the agreement, but I'll feel better if I know you've arrived."

"Okay, Mom. Love you."

"I love you too, my darling. God bless you."

He has, I want to tell her. *It isn't nearly as pleasant as you might think.*

VI.

My advisor's friend is supposed to meet me at the bus station, but I don't see anyone who matches the image I have of him. I wait until the station clears of everyone except people waiting for some other bus to come.

I'm looking for someone who looks like my advisor, who still wears his military service proudly—buzz-cut hair, ramrod posture. Instead, half an hour later, a short, round man with a flowing Civil War–style mustache bustles through the depot. He looks like a cross between Colonel Sanders and an Oompa-Loompa.

"I'm Frank," he says as I stand there, my legs stiff and my back sore from the long ride. "Frank Hale. You must be Miriam. And aren't you a pretty little thing. Hope you haven't been waiting long." He looks around with a moue of distaste. "Can't say the bus station is our most *attractive* site. Maybe it's time for the city council to step in."

"It's nice to meet you," I say.

We shake hands, and he holds on a second longer than necessary before reaching for my suitcase.

"Come along," he says, as if I have been dawdling. "Let's get to the car and I can show you around a bit."

I slide into his giant white Cadillac and brace myself as he presses the gas too hard in reverse. The car leaps out of its parking spot like it was stung by a bee. A quick three-point turn later and we're headed on a two-lane road toward Hamilton.

After fifteen minutes, we enter the town limits and pass a sign that reads HAMILTON, THE BEST LITTLE TOWN IN TENNESSEE! CIVIL WAR HERITAGE SITE. It seems clear the two are related.

Frank, meanwhile, is busy telling me all about my new hometown.

"We film commercials on Main Street about once a month. Folks around here love it. Sometimes they need extras, and you should see the lines in front of the casting tent. They do close down the road to car traffic, and that causes a stir from the local businesses. Still, it's a bonanza for the town, no mistake about that. Once there was a movie with Johnny Depp that paid for a ten-mile biking trail from the park to the county rec center by the river. He was a nice fellow, that Johnny Depp. An odd duck, mind you, but nice enough . . ."

I'm exhausted from the bus trip, and his chatter soon fades into background noise.

I wake with a start when the car rocks to a stop. We've parked in front of a small yellow building two blocks off the famous Main Street and, according to Frank, not far from the newspaper. Frank hefts my big suitcase and I follow him with my backpack. He unlocks a door and shows me a small one-bedroom apartment. It's furnished, it's clean and it's mine. I love it.

"Now, the gal that lives here got herself a one-year internship in Paris, so I know she'll be mighty glad to have someone look after the place."

And pay her four-hundred-dollar-a-month rent, I think, but don't say that.

"What is she doing in France?" I ask, half jealous despite myself. Some girls get a low-paying job in small-town Tennessee; some apparently snag a job in Europe.

"France?" he says, confused. "Now, why would she go there? She's in Georgia. Paris, Georgia. She's doing something with real estate development. Some sort of partnership between us and them."

"Oh. That's nice." The bemused look on my face draws him out of his ramblings. "Hon, you look tuckered out. Why don't you rest here, settle in, do a bit of exploring over the weekend, and report to work bright and sharp on Monday."

"Okay," I say, unbearably weary. "That sounds great. Thanks for everything."

"Welcome to Hamilton," he says. He pats my arm and leaves.

I flop on the bed, grateful that it's made and that the pink flowered sheets smell clean. I managed to mumble through the Birkat Habayit, the blessing for the home, and the Shehechiyanu, the blessing for new events, which roughly translates as: "Thank you, Lord our God, for giving us life, and sustaining us, and bringing us to this day." I'm still feeling my way around everyday prayer, trying to figure out how much is expected of me, what is a fair prayer. I learned the Shehechiyanu and Birkat Habayit as part of my bat mitzvah training, long evenings sitting at the kitchen table with my father, repeating the Hebrew words after him. Mo hated studying for his bar mitzvah. Only the thought of the massive amount of presents and money he'd miss out on without a bar mitzvah kept him going. As it was, we split the Torah portion reading between the two of us. He took the first three verses, all short, while I chanted the last four, which were twice as long. But I didn't mind. When I was with Mo, I pretended I hated studying Hebrew too. But when it was only my father and me, sitting in the bright kitchen while night grew heavy outside, we would have the most wonderful discussions about the meaning of a vowel in a word, the trop on a word, the choice of a pronoun or a repeating adjective. Every strange mark, every odd choice, was meaningful to him.

Both my parents looked at religion as a powerful and meaningful way to structure one's life. My father saw Judaism's interest in details as a form of worship. The particles of meat that could be left over on a washed plate and mingle with the next meal's cheese meant that there were separate dishes for meat and dairy to honor the mandate that one should not cook a calf in its mother's milk.

My mother's Catholicism meant she turned to Jesus in her

daily life: we owed him an impossible debt for saving us from original sin and he looked on us with kindness and mercy. Sins could be and were forgiven with proper repentance, and we must love and serve God in this world.

Neither of them ever lost sight of the fact that God was the creator of all things: the sun, the moon, dancing honey-bees, pregnant sea horses, and all the other wondrous creatures that live on earth.

I see now that attention to detail would have helped prevent the pickle I'm in now. I hope that I can be forgiven. My repentance is sincere.

Their shared belief that God is interested in all things great and small—the tiniest detail and the incomprehensible concept of an expanding universe and black matter—leaves me frightened about what will happen to Mo.

I worry and nibble on a fingernail. I'm not sure what I can do about his enchantment with the devil. We've texted and e-mailed this past week, but despite his excitement and assurances, I don't buy his conviction that the devil isn't all bad. I remember the heated arguments he and my dad would get into around the time of his bar mitzvah, Mo claiming that the Bible was the world's bestselling novel, a great adventure story but a silly book to base your life on; my father, eyes flashing, insisting that the Bible is the word of God. Has meeting the devil only reinforced Mo's belief that God is irrelevant?

Tired as I am, thinking about my father reminds me I'm supposed to check in. I call him and ask that he tell my mom about my safe arrival.

"I said two prayers when I arrived," I tell him. There is a pause, and I wish I could see the expression on his face. "It seemed like the right thing to do."

"B'sha'ah tovah," he says, which literally means "in a good hour" but is used to say "Congratulations!" I can't tell if he's being sarcastic. It always strikes me as odd how he is so devout and so cynical at the same time.

"Okay, Dad. Don't forget to tell Mom."

"I won't. Love you, sweetheart," he says. The kindness and love in his voice make me doubt the earlier snarkiness I thought I detected. "Take care of yourself."

I've never been much for praying, but those two prayers felt right. Call me crazy, but I suspect there's more than an even chance that divine intervention brought me here. It seems like a good idea to appreciate that, for the moment, it's a benign, pain-free intervention. I know how quickly and easily that can change.

My job at the *Hamilton Morning Gazette* is part errand girl, part copy editor, part headline writer. The bone of contributing to a story is occasionally tossed my way, usually when a stringer has dropped the ball. I have a day, sometimes two, to catch at least three sources willing to be quoted and to verify facts, write a catchy lead and work with the existing fragment until it resembles a six-hundred-to-nine-hundred-word article. Sometimes I even take the photos that accompany the story.

I tell myself that such a well-rounded introduction to the newspaper business is every cub reporter's dream. Or what they would dream about after the *New York Times* gave their prestigious summer internship to someone else. I'm learning the ropes, top to bottom—though, if I'm honest, mostly bottom. But really, apart from the fact that my salary is so low that after rent and utilities I have about two hundred dollars a month for food and entertainment, I actually like my job.

Within a week of starting at the *Gazette*, I meet the mayor. He eats every morning, at seven o'clock sharp, at the Rise and Dine, a local breakfast spot. Armed with that bit of information, I accost him like a true reporter. Though unlike one, all I do is shyly say hi and introduce myself. I like the mayor, an affable middle-aged father of four who is an insurance salesman by trade. He seems to have the perpetual look of a man trying to recall some minor piece of news that slipped his mind.

Judge Bender, the county judge I meet on Wednesday, has the look of a man who hasn't finished digesting a too large meal. He is overweight, with a bullfrog-like bulge that marries his chin to his neck. He has fluffy white hair and the complexion of a drinker. His round face is ruddy except for a raccoon patch of pale skin around his eyes, like that of a boater or skier, which is odd on a man from a landlocked state with hardly any snow. I don't like the flare of interest I see in his eyes when Frank introduces us. I feel like a piece of pie he is eyeing for dessert.

That's about it for the town pillars I meet during my first week.

On Frank's orders, I explore Hamilton. Although I grew up in a southern state, living in a university town blunted the impact of true southern life. Coming to Hamilton, I have entered the heart of southern charm, hospitality and quirkiness. The gushy friendliness on the streets, the thick accents, charm me to bits.

Spring is blooming and it seems every patch of dirt had tulip and iris and daffodil bulbs hidden in it. Pansies flash their colored faces from window boxes, and the trees are heavy with pale pink and white blossoms.

There are a lot of antique stores in Hamilton, their display windows full of down-home, country-cute decorations. Antiquing is a sport here, and it shows. I poke around in a few stores, but I don't get the appeal. The overpriced merchandise repeats itself with astounding regularity. Roosters, large tin stars, gingham curtains and angels. Angels are very popular here. Every time I pass a sun-faded angel garden statue or a hand-painted pastel sign about guardian angels, I shudder.

I look over my shoulder and wait for the other shoe to drop.

I wonder if this is what a Mob suspect feels like right before the FBI swoops in to make an arrest.

VII.

TWO WEEKS INTO MY LIFE in Hamilton and more than a month since Raphael spoke to me and no shoes have dropped, nor have any other angels popped in for a visit. On the other hand, I already have a favorite coffee shop and know the librarian and the postman by name.

Although working and living here feels like the calm before the storm and I know I'm not out of the woods, I like Hamilton. It's already grown to be less of a random spot to crash for a few months and more like the kind of place I want to stay for the foreseeable future.

I feel pleased with myself when I find a shortcut between Main Street and the library by cutting down a couple of alleys and hurrying through a slightly shabby neighborhood. It's only a few blocks long, but unlike the cottage-like perfection of those near Main Street, this neighborhood has homes that look more . . . authentic. The lawns are ragged, with large patches of dandelions and clover. The paint on the houses' siding is either peeling or speckled with mold. There are a few commercial properties intermixed with residential ones: a mechanic's shop, a pawnshop and a tattoo parlor. Though the houses are tiny, many have been converted into duplexes and apartments.

Hamilton is too small and quaint to have slums, but if it did, then this tiny stretch would qualify, though there's no sense of menace or danger, just a tired lack of wealth. Several of the buildings on Main Street have strange green and yellow flags displayed this morning, and as I head to the library, I see one of them hanging on a decrepit-looking Victorian with four mailboxes nailed next to its peeling front door. I wonder why the town elders haven't insisted on sprucing up the place. Perhaps there's an article here.

Then, in the middle of a thought about getting a quote from the mayor on the scarcity of low-income housing, my bowels clench, my face turns clammy, and I suddenly need a bathroom. *Immediately.* I scan the street for a restaurant, a gas station—anything that might have a public restroom.

I haven't had this kind of urgency since grade school. I press my knees together, fighting a wave of panic as I try to think.

The pawnshop is locked and the mechanic's shop looks abandoned. I eye a big oak behind one of the more dilapidated houses but decide that I can't do that. The only thing remotely possible is to try the tattoo parlor two houses away. But if I don't hurry, I'll soil myself. The urgency is so horrible I nearly weep. In an instant I feel less than human. But the terrible need to go is too strong for embarrassment. Gripping my purse tightly, I race to the tattoo parlor and breeze inside.

I have no time for chitchat, no time to waste.

I take in the hundreds of designs pinned up on the wall. I see a couple of empty dentist-like chairs, a long counter with shelves and supplies behind it. Music from a local rock station is playing, while an underlying buzz that sounds like a dentist's drill comes from a far corner, where I assume a tattoo is in progress. The most likely place for a bathroom is in the back, and I stride in that direction as if I have every right to.

"Hey, guys," I say lightly, shooting a glance at the tattoo artist and his victim, a thin guy with wispy facial hair getting his calf tattooed. "Is there a bathroom here?"

"Straight back," says the tattoo artist, bent over his work and not looking up. "Past the curtain."

"Great," I say, never breaking stride. "Thanks."

I brush aside the curtain, mentally blessing the incurious, straightforward answer while frantically searching in the dim light for a bathroom door. The first one I open is to a supply closet. I bite my lip to keep from moaning. My legs start shaking from the strain. I have no time. The second door leads to a bathroom. I slam the door shut, not even bothering to lock it. Fumble with my panties. Stagger to the toilet in the nick of time.

Afterward, I lean against a midnight-blue wall, waiting for the pain and nausea to pass, for my legs to stop shaking.

I wash my hands, then cup water in my hands and sip,

feeling the cool, metallic liquid slide all the way down my throat and into my quivering stomach. I close my eyes and try to regroup. With heavy certainty, I know that something is terribly wrong with my body. It's an unnerving, frightening thought. Is there an official prayer for "Oh shit, what the hell am I supposed to do now?"

I take a shuddering breath and realize I'd better not stay in the bathroom too long; it was weird enough for me to come in here like I did. Squaring my shoulders, I practice smiling and go back to the main room of the parlor.

The buzzing has stopped, so the tattoo must be finished. The facial-hair guy admires a heavy black cross floating in a rectangle of conspicuously shaved skin in the middle of his calf. The skin around the tattoo is red and puffy.

Are my new symptoms my very own cross to bear? It's a devastating thought, and one I am unable to deal with in public, in front of strangers. So, for the moment, I push it away.

"Yeah, that's it, man," says Facial Hair in front of a large, floor-length mirror, his eyes on the reflection of the cross. "That's exactly what I wanted. Thanks."

"Good," says the tattoo guy, carefully covering the cross with a gauze square, then snapping off his protective black gloves. "Take care of it. No sun. No scratching. Keep it clean and wash it every day, but don't let the water pound on it—it could smear the ink."

The two shake hands. Then Facial Hair pulls the hood of his sweatshirt up over his head and walks out. A bell jingles as the door closes.

The tattoo artist dons a new set of gloves and starts cleaning his station. He's probably seven or eight years older than me, tall and shaved bald. Tattoos cover his arms from his short-sleeved black T-shirt to his wrists; tattoos curve down his neck and disappear under his collar. I can't see if the rest of him is as inked as his arms, since he's wearing jeans and heavy motorcycle boots. The black rubber gloves somehow suit him better than his natural skin.

In my pink sundress and strappy heels, I couldn't look more out of place.

"Thanks," I say. "It was an emergency."

"Yeah, I noticed."

My face flushes, though his tone is dry, not mocking. I should leave. He turns away and pitches used towels in a medical waste bin. The rock station plays a live recording of "Hotel California." The ceiling fans create a light breeze, and I don't feel like walking out. I can't stop watching him. I can see muscles through his thin shirt, rippling and flexing as he bends over the chair, wiping it down.

"I guess crosses are pretty popular around here," I say, walking closer to him and leaning a hip against an adjacent black vinyl chair. I feel a strange pull toward him; there's something elemental about him that is fascinating. Hamilton is charming and welcoming, but there is no denying that people like to live on the surface here. The pleasant, happy surface. The tattoo artist radiates something deeper and darker. Something true.

"Yeah."

"Do you have one?"

He looks up for a second. He has dark brown eyes, almost black. "No."

"You don't need to look so shocked," I say, though it seems there's little that would shock him.

He snorts.

"It's not like there's anything wrong with wanting a cross on your leg. I mean, it's a little egotistical, but the intention is nice." I probably sound spiteful, because he looks at me oddly. I suddenly feel the same constraint I have felt ever since Raphael's visit: that I must watch my words. Is it wrong to make jokes about the cross? I'm not certain how celestial intervention works, but I suspect it involves paying close attention to the terrestrial subject, which in this case is me. Is someone up there keeping tally of all my sins? When they reach a certain number, do I irrevocably lose? Everywhere I go, I feel eyes watching me, ears listening, minds judging.

"So, can you tattoo yourself, or do you have to find someone to do you?" I ask, changing the subject.

He looks at me again, and I start laughing. "I didn't mean it like that." I am a little surprised at myself. The teasing, the one-sided conversation. This isn't like me. It's like Mo.

I sneak quick looks at his arms. At first glance they're a mess of snaking lines, colors, forms melting into one another. But the more I look, the more the tattoos come together into something that almost makes sense, the way the longer you look at clouds, the more familiar shapes you find. I find a dragon, Maori designs, a battle-ax, a dogwood blossom.

"I don't mean to bother you," I say, remembering that I'm usually shy with strangers. He hasn't said much as he's cleaned up his station, and I suddenly wonder how this looks from his perspective. Flirting and ogling are clearly not my strong suit. I reluctantly push myself to stand. "You're probably busy."

"Not really," he says. "It's quiet today." Maybe I'm reaching, but I sense a peace offering there. I wonder if he's lonely.

"I'm Miriam," I say, extending a hand.

"Emmett Black." We shake. His hand is warm, his grip strong but very gentle. It feels ridiculously nice. I let go with a palpable sense of regret.

"So, Emmett Black." I sit down in the chair because I'm tired of standing and because I want to know more about him. "How long have you lived in Hamilton?"

"Couple of years. You?"

"Couple of weeks. I like it. It's different here."

He laughs. "Really? I hadn't noticed."

"Sure," I say. "It's so cute and perfect, with this glaze of southern charm over it. People try to be so much like what they're *supposed* to be that it makes them a little crazy. It's the reason I decided to live here. That and the job offer." And the small matter of fleeing a terrifying encounter with the divine, but never mind about that.

"Where do you work?"

"At the *Morning Gazette*. I'm a writer, copy editor, chimney sweep—basically, if it needs to be done, I'm the person to do it. Except for selling ad space. I am not a salesperson."

"No, I can see that."

I look to see if he's making fun of me and decide that he is, but not in a bad way.

"What brought you to the tattoo business? I'm not being

60

nosy," I say before he can answer. "I'm doing my job. We do profiles on prominent and/or interesting citizens."

"You think I qualify?" His deep voice carries amusement, skepticism and a hint of resentment.

"Now you're just fishing for compliments," I say. That surprises a laugh out of him, which pleases me no end.

But he doesn't have a chance to answer, because the bell jingles behind me. We both turn to see two giggling college girls walk in, standing close and bumping into each other for strength.

"How can I help you?" he says. It's only when he steps toward them that I realize how close he's been standing to me.

"Hi," one says uncertainly, glancing at him, then at me. "Um, we wanted to get matching tattoos." They both start giggling again.

"Yeah, you know"—giggle, giggle—"tramp stamps."

Emmett looks serious as he listens to the description of the tattoo.

"I can sketch you something. Come back in an hour."

"Oh." They're clearly disappointed and shoot another quick appraising glance in my direction. "We can't, you know, do it now?" I wonder if they think I'm his girlfriend.

"If you picked flash, I could do it now. But if you want something original, then I have to draw it first," he explains patiently.

A furious discussion ensues, with lots of giggling, hair-twirling and lip-biting.

"He's got mad skills," I pipe in with conviction. Come back in an hour, I think, I'm not finished talking with him yet. Emmett doesn't look my way, but I feel he's hiding a smile.

The girls roll their eyes, but it's settled: they decide they would rather have an "original design." I can tell how much it pleases them to phrase it that way, and I can almost hear them talk about it at the next party they go to. An *original* design. *One of a kind.* Except they're both going to get the same one: two daisies tied together with a ribbon. The design might be original, but the concept is hackneyed.

The bell jingles as they leave and we're alone in the shop again. An old Indigo Girls song comes on, their deep, raspy voices harmonizing about a faithless lover.

"Thanks for the endorsement," he says. "I didn't realize you were such a fan of my work."

"How long before they have a great big fight and aren't speaking to each other anymore?" I ask, ignoring his ironic tone.

"Six months."

"That was a rhetorical question."

"And no," he says. "I don't feel bad that the tattoo will be there forever, long after they're not friends."

"I didn't say that."

"But you were thinking it," he says in that deep voice. "Everyone does. What a tattoo does is capture a moment. It's there with you, a part of you, long after the moment is gone and the memory fades."

"That's nice," I say. "But don't come crying to me when they sue you."

Again, I feel almost proud when he laughs.

"I should let you get back to work," I say, sliding reluctantly off the seat. "Today just got a little less quiet."

"Come back and use the bathroom anytime," he says—an understated invitation to return.

"Thanks." I smile. "I will."

The bell jingles behind me as I go, leaving him to his sketching.

Thinking how nice it was to talk with him, I realize that I am desperate to pretend I'm normal and healthy and not stalked by angels, punished by God.

Yet even without shoes dropping or angels visiting, just the thought of that icy clear light, that terrible voice, makes me feel weak and ill. I glance over at the quiet haven of the tattoo shop, which seems like a bastion of normalcy even as it projects a sense of urban edginess in this quaint little town. And just like it forces Hamilton to acknowledge that it is no longer the 1950s, I know that no matter what I want to pretend, the truth is with me. The issue of what drove me into the tattoo parlor is inescapable. I need a doctor, but I fear what I have is nothing a mortal can fix.

As my mother said when we were younger and faced unpleasant consequences, my chickens had come home to roost.

I shiver, though the day is pleasant and warm.

I begin my walk to the newspaper office, wrapped in melancholy.

VIII.

ON MY WAY TO THE NEWSPAPER OFFICE, I notice the strange flags again. Bright yellow with a large green *H*. I can't figure out what they have to do with anything. City Hall doesn't have one, but the bank, two restaurants and a high-end boutique do. The courthouse doesn't, but a couple of law firms do. A few private homes have them, though most don't.

Frank's in his office, so after peeking in to make sure he isn't on a phone call, I enter.

"Is there a festival or something?" I ask him.

"What?"

"The *H* flags—what's that about?"

He leans back in his seat far enough that it creaks, and I hope it doesn't break under the strain. "It's the one hundred forty-fifth anniversary of the Battle of Hamilton. One of the bloodiest mornings in the history of the war," he says, rather proudly. "Ten thousand dead in three hours." The glee in his voice creeps me out. I'm not a Civil War buff, but I did study it in American history and I never heard of the Battle of Hamilton. All that blood didn't even buy it a place in the history books.

"The *H* is for Hamilton?"

"*H* is for hospital, Miriam. After the battle was over, twenty-eight makeshift hospitals were set up. The battle was fought all around the town. Every house still standing was turned into a hospital."

"Where did they get doctors from?"

"No doctors. Maybe one or two medics rushing around and sawing off limbs. Mostly it was the lady of each house, using up her linens, drawing water, giving comfort as boy after boy died from their wounds. You've seen the cemetery, right? The one behind the Linden Plantation?"

My chest feels tight, and sweat pools under my arms. More proof of God's distant disinterest. How could such terrors exist? This town no longer seems so cute and quaint. I think of all the buildings I pass every day and the horror that occurred in them. I'd seen glimpses of the old cemetery with its small faded markers, its maple trees and wildflowers, and thought it a peaceful place.

"Think of it, Miriam," Frank continues. If nothing else, the man loves a good story. "Boys your age dying as their legs were sawed off with no anesthesia, bleeding to death or, worse, rotting from the inside out from gangrene. No antibiotics then, remember."

"Yeah, I knew that," I say weakly. And where was Raphael

then, that cold healing angel? Where was the meddling, the divine concern that has landed me in this current situation? Once again, I'm shocked and frightened to be singled out like this.

"They were burying them as fast as they could dig. It was the last Southern offensive of the war. After that battle the Yankees took the initiative, so to speak. You all right there?"

"Yeah," I say, knowing I look pale. "Gruesome, though."

"Nothing like history to give you a bit of perspective, eh? Now, was there something you wanted?"

For a second I've forgotten what I came here for. Then my stomach cramps up and I remember.

"I might be coming down with a bug or something. Do you have the name of a good doctor?"

"Poor thing," he says, instantly solicitous. "I'm so sorry to hear that. Dr. Robert's a great young doc, one of the best in town. He's my aunt's neighbor. You tell him I sent you."

In my cubicle, keeping my voice down, I make an appointment.

But even with the name-dropping, the soonest Dr. Robert can see me is in two weeks. I try to convince myself that by the time the appointment comes around, I will be all better. I can always cancel.

On Saturday Frank sends me to the farmers' market to meet and mingle with the hippie/yuppie/family crowd. It's my first story assignment. Until now I've interviewed a few sources for the other stringer on the paper and done a bit of research. Frank, in his dramatic fashion, declared me ready for the responsibility. The fact that Alex, the other reporter, is off for a couple days isn't mentioned by either of us.

I call my mom and tell her that next week I'll have an article.

"Really?" The delight in her voice zings across the phone line and straight to my toes. "Are they online? Maybe I can subscribe—do you think they would mail me copies?"

"Don't get so excited," I say, though I can't help grinning. "It'll just be a little fluff piece in a tiny little paper."

"Nonsense," she says. "It's your first professional piece and you're only eighteen."

"Cameron Crowe was writing for *Rolling Stone* by the time he was sixteen."

"And what did he ever amount to?" she asks.

"Mom, he's a really famous screenwriter and director."

"I've never heard of him." As if that's supposed to be an inarguable point.

It's funny to me that my friends always liked my dad better than my mom. My dad comes across so cool that no one gave me much sympathy when I complained of the ridiculously high standards he set for my brother and me. My mother was a bit aloof with outsiders, which, combined with her past as a former nun, intimidated my friends. But when it was just us with her, she radiated acceptance. No matter what I did, I could never disappoint her. Both my parents are five foot eight, but while my dad seems taller than his actual height, my mom seems shorter. Something about the way they stand and take up space in a room always makes it hard for me to believe they're the same height. My mom's short gray hair in a perpetual bowl cut contrasts with my dad's messy auburn curls—it's like her hair spurns attention, while his demands it.

My mom didn't like to talk about her life before Dad, but it wasn't a secret that she had been a nun for six years before leaving the order. She'd lost her parents in a car accident when she was five and was raised by a deeply religious uncle. She told me she became a nun at eighteen thinking she'd find the home she'd never had. But like many women who marry young, she and her groom grew apart. Life in a religious order was nothing like she'd imagined. Less *Sound of Music*, more *Big Brother*. At twenty-four, she left the church with a heavy heart. Three years later, when she and my dad got together, she was getting her doctorate in comparative religion, living a completely secular life. She agreed to raise the kids Jewish; hence my bat mitzvah. It was quite a scandal at my dad's congregation when the rabbi married a former nun, a shiksa from England. I'm sure the nuns were equally horrified.

Mom would come with us to synagogue and read from the prayer book, speaking the Hebrew words in her proper English accent. I do believe her commitment was genuine, but as we got older, she rediscovered her Catholic faith. After the divorce, she quietly resumed attending Sunday mass.

Faith is something that seems to imprint on you when you're young. After the divorce, I grew very close to my mom, and part of that meant I went with her to mass. Though my father and I never spoke about it, he must have worried I would convert to Catholicism. But I never found it hard to separate spirituality and dogma. Being raised Jewish had taken hold, and even after my mom began attending mass regularly, even after I started going with her, I enjoyed the spirituality of Catholic service without being confused by dogma.

Obviously the doctrines of the two religions are different, which is why many people can't look past their incompatibility. Perhaps it's because I was raised by parents who found a way to reconcile that conflict that I found myself attracted to the sense of quiet gratitude for the beauty and preciousness of life that is such a big part of both services. Catholic worship is also a visual feast. The beautiful stained-glass windows, the robes—even the churches themselves—create a sense of peaceful serenity. I understood why my mother craved it. Nothing else must have ever felt quite right to her. The songs, the words, the language, weren't the same, but after a few years of reciting the same prayers side by side with my mother, I found the same comfort, the same peacefulness, the same sense of hope that I found from chanting the Kaddish or the Shema in synagogue.

As I hang up the phone, it occurs to me again that if I told my mom the reason I left school, if I told her about Raphael's visit, she would believe me. I'm not sure if this is a flaw or not, but my mom always believes whatever Mo and I tell her. It used to be a game we played, to tell her outrageous stories about the things we saw on the way to school, the people we met. She would listen and ask questions and never seem to doubt the possibility that maybe we didn't really meet the president of the United States at school or weren't really invited to join the NASA program as the first children in space. When I started to giggle and Mo would admit we were "just teasing" or "making a joke," she would laugh right along with us. The one time we fooled my dad, telling him we'd been expelled from school for refusing to take communion—this was a public school, mind you—he was angrier at the fact that we tricked him than at the thought that the school had mandatory communion.

But I don't tell my mom the truth. For one, it seems much too late to start admitting I met an angel. For another, not telling anyone (except Mo, and he doesn't count) hasn't gotten me into trouble. What if telling my mom brings the angel back? What if this time he's angry? It was bad enough to meet him for a routine—if that's what you can call it—assignment. Having an encounter where he's angry just might kill me.

The thought that I am being punished bubbles up from the dark, bitter part of my mind, but I brush it aside.

When I call my dad for our weekly check-in, my unhappiness with God comes up in a sort of vague, theoretical way.

"Doubt is built into Judaism," he says as soon as I tell him I'm struggling. I don't explain that it isn't my faith that's wavering, it's what to do about my newfound religiosity. "The name Israel means 'he who struggles with God.' Notice it doesn't say 'doubts'; it says 'struggles.' The important thing is to *do*, to *act*." My father is passionate about this, and it's obvious it's something he's thought about. His words give me chills. "The rabbis say we're judged by our deeds, not our words—and never by our thoughts. So when you have doubt, when you feel anger or bitterness toward God, no one is marking demerits on your soul."

I wonder when he had his moments of doubt. Perhaps he still does.

"But what if your acts aren't good enough? What if they aren't what God had in mind?" I hope he takes this as a rhetorical question.

"That's just another way of saying you doubt. You can hold on to those feelings, but your actions better be those that follow God's commandments, that help your fellow man. Do any of us reach our full potential? Is there anyone who could say in all honesty that they couldn't have done anything more than they did? No. God has set an impossible standard for us. We're human, fallible, selfish, weak. We do the best we can and live our life. Does that help?"

"No."

We both laugh.

"There's this great old saying I learned in rabbinical school that during the day God dictated the Torah to Moses, and at night He explained it to him." He pauses to let that sink in.

"Then no wonder the rest of us are floundering," I say. "But I guess that makes sense."

"Sure it does," my father says. "Now take care of yourself and call more often. You don't need a crisis to talk to your old man." He sounds lonely, and I feel a zing of guilt for not doing more and calling more often. Another thing to add to my list of inadequacies.

"Yeah, Dad." The phone pressed to my ear is warm. I'm alone in my tiny apartment and I wish my dad were here. "And thanks."

* * *

The Saturday farmers' market is held under a large wooden shelter next to an empty parking lot I'd passed several times during the week without paying much attention to it. Now the lot is so overflowing with cars that there's a crooked line of them on the grass by the side of the road.

I park my car, on loan from Frank. I hear the bluegrass music before I see any produce, and as I hike over to the market, I unintentionally keep time with the lively beat that shakes out from under the massive shelter that houses the market. As I draw closer, I see tables piled with mounds of fresh veggies in shiny pyramids and glorious bunches of wildflowers arranged in bouquets that would make Martha Stewart weep with joy. There are stands selling baked goods, homemade cheeses and crafts. The band, up on a tiny stage, consists of four generations of the Winkler family, as a draping sign proclaims. Toothless Great-grandpa, wearing an I'M THE BOSS baseball cap, plays the bass; Granny and Dad play the fiddle; while the youngest member of the family, a girl of about ten, looks both embarrassed and pleased as she plays the accordion and is sometimes persuaded to sing in a high, clear voice. They sing Civil War–era melodies that must have been sung in this very town for over a hundred years. As I remember the *H* flags from earlier in the week and Frank's graphic recounting, the lovely melodies, and plaintive fiddle seem haunting.

I shake off grim thoughts of war and begin jotting down impressions in the small notebook I've brought with me: the soft morning air, the scent of crushed basil leaves, the unhurried mix of families, dedicated hippies in vegan shoes and conservative social pillars picking through wildflower bouquets probably intended for their evening's dinner parties. I'm trying to stay a detached observer, but the market is such fun that I find myself beguiled by it. I tuck the notebook into a back pocket, as I am unable to resist buying spring baby lettuce, a bright, happy bunch of sunflowers and strawberries that smell like perfume.

A deeply tanned woman in overalls bags my strawberries and we start chatting.

"Yeah, I am new here," I say, answering her question. "I work for the *Gazette*." I love saying that. I tilt a hip so she can see the reporter's pad poking out. "I'm actually on assignment," I say. "But I'm mixing business and pleasure."

Her eyes gleam with interest, so I ask her a few questions about her farm, how long she's been coming to the market and what's in season. Juggling the bag of produce on my arm, I write down her comments. The bags are slipping, but I don't want to hug them too tightly, since the lettuce and strawberries could squish. The flowers keep poking me in the eye. I feel a blush coming on; I must seem like such an amateur. There's a reason mixing business and pleasure is usually a bad idea.

"Your parents must be proud of you, beautiful," she says, giving me a chance to finish writing her last quote.

I look up from my notepad and smile. "Thanks."

"You should come by the farm one day," she says. "Might make a nice story, and even if it doesn't, you'd like it there."

"Really?"

"Sure. We'll put you to work. I can tell you're a city girl. You should see where your food comes from."

"Yeah, I should. I'm Miriam," I say, shifting my packages so we can shake hands.

"Trudy," she says. "That's Hank over there."

She points to a man, wrinkled and tanned, unloading more produce, adding it to their table loaded with big juicy strawberries, long stalks of rhubarb, small mountains of sugar snap peas and a complicated structure of broccoli. He's tall and thin, like a younger version of the farmer in *American Gothic*. He's missing a pitchfork and glasses, and he has a trimmed beard, but he has the same patient look and gaunt frame of the man in the painting. He looks up when he hears his name. I wave.

As I fumble for my wallet to pay for my purchase, Trudy pushes away the money. "This is your welcome present to Hamilton," she says over my protests. "Come to the farm," she says again, and squeezes my hand. She gives me a recipe for tomato-and-cheese pie, assures me it's easy and delicious and turns to help the next person in line.

I leave the market clutching my veggies, my flowers and my first story idea.

I spend the rest of the weekend polishing up the farmers' market piece. I've interviewed a young mom and her three-year-old, his mouth stained bright red from strawberries. A city official has given me a couple of statistics on how much revenue the market brings in, how long it's been active. I move the quotes around in the story, write three different leads and e-mail my favorite three drafts to my mom, my dad and Mo to help me choose which is best. When they e-mail back with opinions and each with a different favorite opening, I spend another couple of hours debating whether to implement their suggestions or not. In the end, I keep the article as I first wrote it.

On Monday, back at the office, I print out the article and show it to Frank. I hold my breath as he skims it, waiting for his reaction. Less than a minute after he's started reading it, he nods and puts it down.

"Good," he says. "We'll run it Friday."

I fight to pull off a blasé face, as if I regularly have articles accepted for publication. From Frank's suppressed smile, I can tell I'm not fooling anyone.

"I think there's another story there," I say with studied casualness. "That vendor I quoted from Sweetwater Farm is local. It's the only CSA farm in the county."

Frank, now clicking at something on his computer screen, utters a distracted "Hmm?"

"It's where people pay for the farm costs and then get a share of the harvest. It's all organic. All local."

He stops typing and thinks for a second. "Are they hippies?" he asks suspiciously.

"Only a little."

His tongue pokes around his mouth. He sucks his teeth. I hold my breath.

"Yes, it could work," he finally says. "Is it safe to presume you'd like to cover this?"

I try to play cool, but my whole face lights up in excitement. Frank laughs. "I'll take that as a yes."

"Yes!"

"All right, Miriam. Six hundred words. You have until the end of the month."

I float back to my desk, grinning like a fool.

I e-mail Mo and my parents, so excited I can barely stand it. This is even better than my first published piece. This is my first story idea. I shoot Trudy an e-mail with the news and ask for a good time to come over for the interview. Although a lot of reporters interview a subject over the phone, or even by e-mail, the best reporting is done when you meet face to face. Plus, I want to see this farm for myself. I'm too wound up to do interviews for a story on the city council's vote to move trash pickup from Mondays to Tuesdays. I glance through the list of upcoming topics. There's a rumor that the superintendent is considering putting in metal detectors at the local high school. It sounds ridiculous to me in this quaint town, but maybe there's a history of trouble I haven't heard about. I start making notes to research school violence in Hamilton, but before I know it, I get distracted by stupid links and online articles on organic gardening, and then by daydreams of writing a feature on Trudy. I know she won't answer my e-mail immediately, so when I smell a fresh pot of coffee brewing, I head to the break room.

In his mid-twenties, Alex is the closest to my age among the *Gazette*'s staff. Of medium height and with a prematurely receding hairline, he's tanned and lean from the long rambles he takes through the woods, searching for Civil War artifacts. It's an open secret that he's working on a novel about the

Civil War battle that took place in Hamilton—the bloodiest three hours of the war, or whatever Frank had called it.

As we wait for the fresh pot of coffee to finish brewing, I bring up the *H* flags, which leads us to an involved discussion about local history.

"It's so creepy," I tell him.

"What do you mean?"

"I know you're a big Civil War buff," I say. "So I guess you've always felt this connection to the past, but for me it was surreal to walk through town and see all these flags marking basic carnage. It really made me see this place in a different light."

Alex beams approvingly at me, as if I've just signed on to join his church.

"That's exactly it," he says. "Most people don't get it. But everything is built on what came before. And for us here in Hamilton, what came before—and not that long ago—changed the entire course of American history.

"People here take it for granted. They grew up with family stories of the war; it's just a part of who they are. But as an outsider coming here, I can't believe they don't take better care of what they have." Which is when he tells me about his secret: an unexcavated, almost totally unknown Civil War site.

"Can you imagine an entire Civil War Union Army headquarters all grown over, unexcavated? It's not even marked with a National Register of Historic Places sign, and heck, any house built before 1950 can get that. When you walk there, you can practically hear the soldiers, smell the camp-fires." His eyes blaze with the fierce joy I usually expect from religious converts and cult members.

"How do you know about it?" I ask.

"I'd heard people talk about it. It was built by the Confed-erates, then taken over by the Union Army. I knew it had to be near water and pretty close to town. So I started hiking in the general area by the river until I found it. It's not like the locals don't know it's there. They do. They just don't think it's anything special." He shakes his head in bafflement.

Alex tends to monopolize conversations and nearly always talks about the Civil War, but I enjoy chatting with him in the break room. He might be an odd duck, as Frank would say, but he's always friendly and treats me as a fully legitimate reporter. The other three employees are much older than me and, aside from a genial "Good morning," don't waste too much time chatting. Sometimes there's a high school intern lurking about, but every couple of months it's a new kid, and this month's kid bailed after a week. A new intern starts soon, and I wonder if we'll get along or if it'll be weird to have someone basically my age around who's an intern while I'm a full-time employee.

"In all the time I've hiked there, I've never seen anyone else," Alex says. "I'm writing up a grant proposal, going to see if I can't get UT students to come excavate it."

The coffee machine sputters, signaling the brewing process is complete. I wait as Alex pours himself a mug of the awful stuff. Even fresh, it tastes bitter and slightly burned. He douses it with creamer, then rips open two packets of sweetener, dumping them in for good measure.

"The fact that it's abandoned and forgotten, that's freaking incredible." I've lost track of the conversation, and it takes me a moment to realize he's still talking about the Union headquarters. Even for Alex, this has been a remarkably long exegesis. "It's what every Civil War buff dreams of, to discover something like that. But it's too important. It belongs on the National Register."

A part of me wants to tell him that we already know all about the Civil War, that it's not like we need to dig up clues to figure out who won or how they did it, but I don't want to hurt his feelings.

"Next time you go, I'll come with you," I say. Though his excitement is a bit silly, there's something about his description of the place that's compelling. New in town with no friends, I'll volunteer to tag along on just about anything.

"You're a sweetheart, Miriam," he says, smiling. Is he flirting with me? Ugh. I hope not. Hopefully he sees me as a surrogate kid sister. "If you want to go, then I'll give you directions. It's an amazing place, and the first time you go there, you really should go alone. It's like"—he searches for the perfect word—"holy. Like it's sacred."

I break out in goose bumps at his careful choice of words.

He pulls out his reporter's notebook and quickly scrawls directions, even sketching me a crude map. I admire his skills. I haven't gotten the hang of fast note-taking, as my bumbling at the farmers' market showed.

Alex rips out the page, but before he hands it over, he makes me swear not to excavate or remove anything I find: bullets, buttons, coins. Secret diaries of the commanding officer.

I promise.

"By the way," I say casually. "Can you recommend a good doctor?"

He pauses in the act of taking a sip, lips comically pursed. "Are you okay?" He looks concerned, but I notice that he leans back a bit.

"Sure," I say. "It's nothing contagious. I just have a couple of questions." I want to see someone soon, and the appointment with Frank's doctor is still over a week away.

"I'll ask around," he says, and hustles out of the small room, suddenly anxious to get back to his computer. He doesn't realize I can see him at his desk as he squirts his hands with antibacterial gel and pops a couple of vitamin C tablets. Trying not to feel insulted and plague-ish, I add "hypochondriac" to Alex's list of quirks.

Four days later, it's my birthday. Our birthday. The phone rings at 7:31 in the morning, the time Mo and I were born nineteen years ago.

"Happy birthday, darling," my mom says, her crisp British accent lovely to hear.

"Thanks." I rub my eyes, trying to wake up. My mother never has understood how anyone could sleep past dawn. She'd probably been up for hours. Seven-thirty-one, she'd always felt, was a decent enough time to call. Too bad she's still early by about three hours.

"You have any special plans for today?"

"Actually, I do. I have the day off. I'm going to hike to an old Civil War site someone at work told me about." And I'll be getting an earlier start than I planned.

"That odd Alex fellow?" I'd described all my co-workers for her.

"He said it was really awesome. I have the day off, so I figured I'll go exploring."

"Sounds like a lovely birthday plan. Make sure you bring your cell phone with you. Have you talked with Mo yet?"

"I just woke up."

"I haven't been able to reach him. He's been difficult to get hold of lately." My mother is not a nudge. If she was complaining about it, that meant she hadn't reached Mo in days of trying. This makes me very uneasy, but I shrug it off.

"You know Mo," I say. "He probably forgot to charge his phone and he can't figure out why no one's calling him. Besides, it's close to finals time, so he might have holed up in the library." This would be very unlike him, but neither one of us says that.

"You're probably right. Happy birthday again, my darling dearest. And make sure you call your brother, okay?"

After we hang up, I sit in bed, staring at my phone. Finally, with a deep sigh, I dial Mo's number. It's a bit early for him, but maybe that means he'll be too groggy to think about dodging the phone.

The phone rings so many times I'm certain his voice mail will pick up, but eventually a bleary voice growls, "Wha' the hell?"

"Happy birthday, brother," I say in my chirpiest voice.

"Christ," he says. There's silence for a moment, and I can almost feel him pulling himself together. "What time is it?"

"Almost eight. In the morning, in case you've lost track."

"Har, har. Some of us have to stay up late studying for *school*. Remember that? Professors? Papers? Final exams?"

"And some of us get up early for *work*," I jab back.

That gets a laugh out of him. A slightly nasty chuckle that tells me his guilt trip is completely fabricated.

"So, have you had anything interesting happen lately?"

"Work is good. My first piece came out, the one I e-mailed you about, and I have another interview set up—"

"Miriam," he interrupts me. "Don't shit with me. You know what I mean."

"Don't be rude," I say. With Mo, I never know how he's going to be on the phone. Sometimes he's so chatty I have to spend fifteen minutes trying to extricate myself from the conversation. Other times he's curt and unbearably rude, except that I know him well enough to know he doesn't even realize it, he's just too busy in his head.

"You're not answering my question," he says in a singsong voice.

"Fine. No. Nothing *interesting* has happened. Thank God." I wince at my choice of words. I wouldn't call my physical ailments interesting. Nasty, disturbing, painful, but not interesting. Besides, it's clear this has become a business call for Mo, not a personal one. One celestial medium to another.

"Really?"

"Really. And you're starting to piss me off," I say.

"Because you don't like keeping secrets from me," he says in a reasonable voice. "And you're keeping one right now. I can tell. I always know when you're not telling me the truth."

"Oh, shut up." He might be able to tell when I'm leaving something out, but I can tell that he's hiding something too. The hyper attitude, the aggressive questions. He's covering, and it's something I don't want to know about. I immediately feel guilty for that uncharitable thought. He might not be up to anything bad. . . . I feel constricted by the twin weights of worry and fear. "Happy birthday, Mo, I have to go. Call Mom!"

"*And many more* . . . ," he sings in a wobbly, grating voice.

After a morning of errands, I pack a couple of protein bars, a bottle of water and a cell phone. Thus armed, I head out.

The woods start at the outskirts of Greenbrier Park. I walk past the playground, the baseball diamond and the grassy field. There's a small wooden bridge over a brown creek, and I head there, following a path that grows narrower and shaggier as I hike away from the park. The bright sunshine fades, filtered through a green canopy of pine, maple, and oak trees. It's a bit cooler in the shade, slightly damp with the loamy scent of soil, decomposing leaves and thriving colonies of large white mushrooms. At first rustling leaves and sudden bursts of gray blur startle me, but I get used to the squirrels.

Apart from slapping at the occasional mosquito, I don't have much to keep my mind from straying as I hike. I'm not really a nature girl. Other than in my mom's backyard full of cheery black-eyed Susans, purple echinacea and other butterfly-friendly flowers, I don't spend much time outdoors. I should be enjoying myself, calmed by the lack of concrete, trash and noise pollution, but instead I'm antsy. I can't shake the feeling that something isn't right. I jump and twitch as I run into a spiderweb, and I shake my head uncomfortably, slapping at imaginary tickles that may or may not be a blood-sucking tick skittering down my shirt.

I worry about Mo, about what's really going on with him and what I'm supposed to do about it. I want to stroll, savoring and reveling in "the beauty of nature" like everyone says you're supposed to, but instead I find my legs moving faster and faster, hurtling along at something close to a run. I slap again at a tickle on my arm, this time killing a mosquito and leaving a bloody smear. Worrying about Mo is like trying to solve those impossible logic riddles, the ones with no right answer.

The path is narrow but fairly easy to follow. I lose it a couple of times, but Alex's map and directions are remarkably accurate. If Alex hadn't told me there was a destination to the path, I wouldn't have followed it so far away from town. My heart beats disturbingly hard and fast.

Mo's in my thoughts like a drumbeat of doom. His encounters cannot end well. His cocky attitude and his life-long ability to scam and charm have blinded him to the real dangers of his situation.

My thighs are burning from the unusual exertion, and sweat beads and itches on my face and back. Alex said it was about a two-mile hike to the ruins. I'm certain I've gone far-ther than that and that I've probably missed it when I sud-denly come to a clearing.

It's startlingly bright and sunny after the woody gloom of the forest. If I didn't know this was a Civil War site, I might have thought I'd discovered Indian burial mounds. The clear-ing, about the size of a baseball field, has undulating grassy hillocks that form a rough square. There are several outside the square, and five smaller ones inside it. The clearing is at the top of a natural slope, which makes tactical sense if you want to be able to see the enemy sneaking up on you. The creek for drinking and washing must be nearby, but I don't see it.

I sip my water, waiting for my heartbeat to settle. I try to imagine the buildings that used to stand here, but other than the cleared square, which I take to be the main compound, I can't tell what's what. Barracks, maybe? There aren't many hillocks, nor are they large enough to hold more than a hun-dred men or so. They had to keep their food, blankets and weapons somewhere. Storage facilities?

After walking the perimeter and clambering over the mounds, I sit on the grass, my back against a narrow tree, eat my second protein bar and drink the rest of my water. It's peaceful here; my strange restlessness is gone and I'm happy to just watch a few pale yellow butterflies flit among the wild-flowers. How odd that a headquarters from such a bloody war has turned into this peaceful, idyllic spot. I can't hear any cars; I can't see any power lines or litter. Some faint birdcalls and the wind rustling over the long grass and through the trees are the only sounds. There are no unhappy ghosts here. It's simply lovely. There's nothing to hurry back to, so I stretch out in the sunshine, suddenly at ease. I don't have any cramps; I don't have a headache. My legs feel loose and rubbery in a good way, and my breath slips in and out with ease.

I'll figure something out with Mo, I promise myself. I close my eyes, feeling the sun smooth away any lingering tension.

At first the dream is ordinary, butterflies fluttering, but the butterflies gradually turn into something else.

I dream that angels are bustling around, rising up to the sky and back down like busy commuters. They are on a slanted ladder wide enough that some are ascending and some are descending in the organized chaos of a morning commute. The top of the ladder disappears into a misty, whirly bright glow that even in my dream hurts to look at, like the sun in the middle of summer. The closer the angels are to earth, the more solid their forms; the higher they are on the ladder, the more transparent and wraithlike they become, until they fade entirely, becoming part of that impossible blaze at the top.

Each angel holds a ghostly image that fades faster than they do. I can only make out the images near the ground. I recognize Mo and Tabitha, but there is another face that I've never seen before. Some of the angels glance over at me. I see myself lying on the ground, disheveled, against a large boulder.

I assume these are not archangels, since unlike with Raphael, I can bear to look at them—though it probably helps that this is a dream and they aren't speaking to me. I know instantly what I'm looking at. These are angels, and this is Jacob's Ladder. They're busy with each other, a strange, beautiful murmur filling the air as they chat. As is the case with dreams, even though they are not speaking in English, I find their language perfectly understandable. I also find myself in the extraordinary position of eavesdropping on celestial conversations. They are talking about me. None of it is flattering.

"There is beauty in all of creation, but *some* have grace and *some* do not. Have you seen a more wretched creature?"

I hear a chuckle of agreement. They are beautiful, of course. They wear long, draping robes of different colors that float and glide like a dance. They each wear a sash knotted around their waists, the ends of which billow like capes behind the angels who are ascending. The ones descending have their sashes fluttering up as if in a strong breeze, though the afternoon air is warm and still. The branches of the surrounding trees strain toward them, the leaves rippling in their direction; clouds swirl around the ladder.

"That pathetic little form would be difficult to work with, but she does not even try. Look at her hair, so dull and tangled. And short! How dare she change what the Almighty intended to be a flowing mane?"

I want to defend myself, to tell these creatures . . . what? There's nothing for me to say. Their derision feels like physical blows. My sleeping form whimpers and curls into a tight ball. It hurts so much that I expect to see bruises blooming on my skin, hear bones cracking under the pressure. They have more in common with Raphael than I thought.

"And sleeping on a rock like a sloppy little slug. What do

you expect? It was clear long ago that the Chosen were chosen badly."

Someone hisses at that and the voice is silenced,
chastened.

Then all the angels stiffen and straighten, looking at
something above me. I can't see what they're looking at, but
feel a powerful warmth spill over me. My tight muscles relax
so suddenly it's almost like a seizure. Nearly limp, I see my
body flop sideways. I'm forced to agree with the angels. I look
pathetic. Not graceful or lovely. Just a ragged, poorly made
body of a young woman in baggy, unflattering clothes.

A deep, rough voice, loud yet soundless, speaks: *"I WILL
WATCH OVER YOU. I WILL PROTECT YOU AND
GUARD YOU."*

How to describe the voice, except to say that it is a deep,
lyrical compilation of every beautiful thought I have ever had,
every moment of startling beauty. It is a rumbling bass older
than the oldest rock on earth, and it is speaking to me. Each
word forms a shield around me. Love floods into every pore. I
am lovely and precious.

The angels, frozen and humbled, look at my sleeping form
with carefully blank faces. A few bend their heads. One nar-
rows her ice-clear eyes at me. And the one who disparaged
the Chosen looks sick with fear and anger.

I wake up to see the sun settling between the trees, shining
full on my face. I sit up slowly, stunned. Absentmindedly
I flick off several ants that have crawled on my legs during
my nap, though I'm careful not to injure them. I am as

insignificant as an ant, maybe more so, to these angels. And perhaps what goes around comes around faster than you think.

For the first time since Raphael's spring break visit, I realize I have been giving him the benefit of the doubt in assuming that he didn't mean to be so cruel and overwhelming, that he just couldn't help it. Now I wonder if Raphael was cruel on purpose. Angels, it's becoming clear, are no patrons of mankind.

Tucking my crazy, flyaway hair behind my ears, I wince at the tight muscles in my lower back, the knots in my shoulders, the vague but unhappy gurgle in my stomach. Standing carefully, I scan the area, but as before there's nothing to show for my vision. No proof, nothing to cling to, except . . . except that the promise was real. Remembering it, I feel some knots loosen in my neck.

As I walk back through the woods, hurrying home both spooked and calm, I try to sort through the facts. Possibilities and likelihoods, maybes and shoulds and can't-possibly-be's, slip and slide between my fingers, and I can't hold on to anything.

My cell phone rings, a jarring anachronism in the quiet woods. It scares me so badly I cry out in fright and trip, twisting my ankle.

My body shaking in the aftermath of a ridiculous adrenaline surge, I hesitantly flip open the phone. But it's not God. It's Alex.

"I got the name of an internist for you," he says, pride and achievement loud in his voice. "He's new in town—my neighbor says he's the best. His name is Dr. Kreger, and I told the nurse it was an emergency. If you hurry, she said, they could see you this afternoon."

"Oh, thanks." I'm still trying to slow down my racing heart, fighting embarrassment that he said it was an emergency, touched that he cared enough to help out. I can't think for all the mess clanging around in my brain.

"You okay?" he asks after an awkward pause.

"I'm just getting back from the hike you told me about."

"You are?" he crows. "Rock on! Did you love it?"

"It was . . ."—I search for the word—"intense."

"I told you it would be. You didn't disturb anything, did you?"

Only myself, but I don't say that.

"So where's this Dr. Kroger's office?"

"It's Kreger," he corrects me, and then gives me directions. "You really need to hurry; they close at five, but they said if you came right away, they'd squeeze you in. I really laid it on them how sick you are, so they're doing this as a favor. Normally it takes more than a week to get an appointment. So make sure to look pathetic."

I glance at the cell phone and see I have less than thirty minutes to get there. "I'd better run, then," I say. "I'm not back at Greenbrier Park yet."

"Good luck," he says. "See you tomorrow."

I close my phone and begin a slow, semi-urgent lope toward the park. Once again I have completely lost any sense of distance. How far I've gone, how long I have left on this hike, are only vague ideas. Sweat blooms between my shoulder blades, under my arms. Stupidly, I worry about feeling disgustingly clammy when the doctor examines me, and about body odor. As a motivation to run faster, those thoughts are not useful. As a ridiculous distraction to keep me from fretting about a dream of angels and possibly (could it *possibly* be?) God, they work great.

Dr. Kreger's office is located in an industrial part of town I haven't seen much of since I moved here. Car lots, big-box stores and anonymous office buildings line the road like spectators at a parade. As I slow down in Frank's loaner to read the tiny signs in front of various buildings, early commuters honk at me in irritation—southern charm and hospitality only extend so far. I see the number I've been searching for on the other side of the road and veer madly into the turning lane, avoiding a sideswipe accident by a fraction of an inch.

I race out of my car to the building. It's a quarter to five and I fully expect the doctor's office to be locked and the receptionist gone. If they've already seen the last patient of the day, they're not going to bother remaining open for me. But the door is unlocked.

A terse sign on the frosted-glass receptionist's partition warns patients not to knock on it or slide it open, so I write my name and arrival time on the pad of paper. The remaining patients in the waiting room are called by a nurse and disappear into the privileged interior of the office. Eventually the glass rattles aside and a woman peers out.

"You got insurance, sweetie?" she asks.

I hate it when strangers call me "sweetie."

"Sure do, darlin'," I say, hearing the snarl in my tone. She blinks and her face hardens.

"I'll need your card, your driver's license and your co-payment."

After I wait another half hour, a nurse holding a clipboard finally calls my name. I follow her into the examination room, where she curtly tells me to undress and put on a paper dressing gown.

The folded gown is so oddly designed that I can't figure out which side is the front. I take a guess, and feeling very exposed and cold, I sit on the crinkly paper of the examination table and wait another twenty minutes before the doctor comes in. It's surreal to think that an hour ago I lay asleep in the woods, dreaming of angels.

He sits on a stool with wheels, flips through some papers and, without looking at me, asks several questions about my symptoms. Fever? Chills? Aches? Weight loss? He jots down what I say, and when he finally looks up, I realize he seems vaguely familiar. Great.

"Lie back, please," he says.

The paper on the table crinkles under me, and my gown shifts open. I clutch at the front. He pushes around on my abdomen. The whole time, I'm trying to place him. Where have I seen him? I've only been here a few weeks; there aren't that many places I've spent time. The coffee shop? The bookstore? The news office?

I wince as he pushes on a tender spot.

"Does this hurt?"

I nod, then realize he isn't looking at me. "A little," I say.

He taps my belly a few times and it makes a comically woody, hollow sound.

"You can sit up," he says.

His voice isn't familiar at all, just his face. As I sit up, clutching tightly the front of the gown, the sight of my own bare legs jogs my memory of where I've seen him before. He was the guy getting a cross tattoo at Emmett's. Facial Hair.

"From your symptoms, there are several possibilities," he says, looking at his notes as if to refresh his memory. "You probably picked up a parasite, though you might have IBS or IBD or it could be your gallbladder. We can run some stool samples here. But I'm guessing you ate something or drank contaminated fluid. Have you been out of the country lately?"

I shake my head.

"Okay, well, it's still possible that it's a parasite."

I want to ask him about those diagnoses he ran through. I should have brought a pad of paper to take notes. I've never heard of those acronyms, and what could be wrong with my gallbladder? Is that serious?

He swivels on his stool and opens a cabinet door. He hands me a clear plastic cup with a lid. "We'll need you to collect a fecal sample. Bring this back to the nurse."

"I'm supposed to poop in that?" I ask, just to be clear.

He looks surprised at the question. "Yes, it's to collect stool."

He stands up and gives me his hand to shake. His hand feels warm, while mine is icy.

"Someone will call you with the results," he says, and

walks out the door, but then pauses, popping his head back in. "After we get the results, come back and see me." Then he shuts the door behind him.

"But—" I say to the empty room. I don't understand. I was waiting for the part when he asks if I have any questions, because I do. I feel like my mother should be here with me.

After sitting on the examination table for a few moments longer, I hop off and collect my clothing. I remind myself that it doesn't matter what those other "possibilities" are. They don't apply to me, since I probably have a parasite. It sounds gross, but on the other hand, it's likely something easy to take care of. Anybody could pick up a stomach bug. The fact that mine's lasted for more than a month is weird, but what do I know about stomach bugs? There are probably all kinds of bizarre parasites that doctors see all the time.

As I shed the paper gown and hurry into my clothes, I try to figure out why I needed to have stripped in the first place. I can't come up with any plausible reason.

IX.

I TURN IN THE STOOL SAMPLE THE NEXT DAY, humiliated that I'm carrying my own feces in a cup. I put the container inside a little gift bag because, really, what am I supposed to carry my own poop in? Besides, it amuses me to imagine the receptionist going, "Oooh, what's this?" and then going, "Oh, what the *hell* is this?"

Feeling better now that I'm on the cusp of diagnosis and treatment, I decide to pay my favorite tattoo artist a visit during my lunch break.

It's a beautiful day, a perfect foreshadowing of summer. The air is soft and warm, and when I see a couple of butterflies fluttering in the wind like paper flowers, I smile and stand still so that they float and hang in front of me. Despite the frustrating doctor's visit, the expectation of a diagnosis and subsequent cure has me nearly giddy.

My dream is drifting away and has lost some of its power to make me shudder. I know better than to discount it; I can't afford to write it off as a complete figment of my imagination. But there was no task given. Nobody asked me to do a thing, and whatever celestial being blessed me at the end was clearly on my side and is looking out for me. I can live with that.

I arrive at Emmett's tattoo shop. With something close to anticipation, I push open the heavy, old-fashioned door and step inside. A tinkling bell announces me, and this time a haunting Spanish guitar is playing on the stereo. That and the faint clicking and whirling of the ceiling fans are the only sounds in the darkened room.

"Hello?" I call out. No one answers. I step in farther, letting my eyes adjust to the relative gloom. None of the overhead lights are on, and the tinted windows don't let in much light. Figuring Emmett stepped out for a moment, I walk over to a wall and study the sample sketches pinned on it.

Dragons, birds, thorns, wild beasts, team logos, Celtic knots, Maori designs, pinup girls, devils and various flowers all compete for attention. I try to imagine showing up at my dad's with ivy leaf tattoos twining around my arm—the look on his face would be priceless. It's the sort of practical joke Mo would love. He once faked a pierced nose after summer camp. My father got that tight look around his mouth and eyes. It did not go away after the big reveal. As usual, he was more pissed off about the trick than the supposed piercing. So maybe no fake tattoo, let alone a real one.

"Can I help you?"

Startled, I gasp and spin around, feeling like I've been caught snooping.

"You scared me." I press a hand to my hammering heart.

"Miriam," Emmett says, almost smiling. "Have you come for a tattoo?"

"Not today," I say. "Just checking out the art." With his shaved head gleaming in the dim light and his eyes so dark in his face, Emmett should look intimidating. Instead, my heart leaps in a silly glad rush at seeing him again.

"It's called flash."

"Did you draw these—flash?"

"I did some of them, but mainly they're standard flash. Most people need to see a design to be inspired and to know what's considered reasonable." He's wearing another tight black shirt that makes his shoulders look ridiculously broad. Again I try to make out his tattoos without staring too obviously, but they're complicated. I'd need a good overhead light and some uninterrupted time to work them out.

"I like this music," I say. The intricate picking and the haunting melody are an unusual selection for a tattoo parlor. At least it seems that way to me, though I don't spend much time in tat shops. "So, if I were to get a tattoo, what's a good spot?"

"Depends what kind of design you want."

"Something small, nothing painful."

He smiles. "You've never been inked before?"

"I grew up associating tattoos with Holocaust survivors." I shrug. "I never saw them as anything I'd want on my body."

"I redid a concentration camp tattoo once," he says. He

97

straddles a chair, folding his arms across the backrest. He nods his head at the large black vinyl chair next to him. "Sit down, take a load off." I sit and fold my legs under me. The chair is cool, but the thought of him holding a needle and marking my skin makes me break out in a light sweat.

"This guy's grandson brought him in. We reworked the numbers so that they looked like Jacob's Ladder."

"I had a dream about that," I say without thinking.

"A tattoo of Jacob's Ladder?"

"No." A hot blush climbs up my neck and face. "No, about Jacob's Ladder. It was more like a nightmare, actually." My body hurts as I remember the angels' cutting words, the cruel, disgusted look on their perfect, cold faces.

"I'm sorry to hear that," he says.

"So, did those two friends come back for their flowers?"

He thinks for a moment. "Oh, right, the daisy and ribbon. Yeah, they did."

"And?"

"And what? As far as I know, they're still friends." He's so calm and unflappable I really feel like trying to needle him.

"No, I meant, did the design look good on them? Once it's on, it's on forever."

"They were happy with it, which is all that matters."

"Do you have a tattoo that you're not happy with?"

He tilts his head and studies me. I grin at his expression; I don't even feel bad for prying. And though he comes across like such a private person, I know he'll answer me.

"Let's just say there are tattoos that I wouldn't do again. But everything that I've had done was the right decision at the time. They're my map of places I've been." He rubs the side of his neck where part of a tattoo curls up from under his shirt. It seems unconscious, a nervous habit. I wonder if that's one of the tattoos he wouldn't get again. "Not a physical map," he scoffs, misreading my expression. "Not like I got the Coliseum from the time I was in Rome or some shit like that. It's more like the places in my head, my evolution from stupid kid to stupid adult."

His gaze is steady on me, and before long I drop my eyes.

"It's your turn now," he says with a small smile. "What do you regret about your young life so far?"

Immediately an image of Tabitha comes to mind.

"That bad?" he asks softly.

"Pretty much," I say. The flirty mood is gone, completely killed by the reminder that all is not well. That I've failed spectacularly and that quite likely there's more to do, just on the horizon. I think of my future and Mo's with something close to despair.

He considers me for a moment.

"There's a great band in town tonight called Blank Pages," he says. "I've heard them play before, and they're freaking awesome. You want to come?"

"Yeah," I say. Anything, anything, to keep from brooding about my personal disasters. "That sounds fun."

We agree to meet at nine, and of course I try on everything in my closet and find nothing that's both cool and casual. Nothing that says I'm awesome but I don't try too hard. Maybe because such an outfit doesn't exist in this mortal world.

I settle for an old pair of jeans and a black velvet-and-satin top. I think it's a good idea to send mixed messages in an outfit. I'm also under the delusion that the top makes me look older than twelve. I never wear anything with ruffles or bows, or in bright primary colors, because then I really look like an eighth grader.

I half expect Emmett to show up on a Harley; instead, he drives an old but very clean Honda Accord. The day has been warm, but with nightfall the temperature is dropping quickly. The drive is barely ten minutes long and I can't think of anything interesting to say. He parks, and I shiver as I get out of his car.

Since Hamilton is so close to Nashville, it has more music clubs than one would expect in a town of its size, though they mostly cater to the country music crowd. I can't picture Emmett getting down to fiddles and harmonicas.

We step in and I'm deluged by a battery of sensations. The floor is sticky; the air reeks of clove cigarettes and cheap beer. It's dim after the bright lights of the parking lot, and all I see is the indistinct press of bodies.

I don't notice the bouncer at first, and so miss the exchange when he tells Emmett there's a cover charge. By the time I realize who Emmett's stopped to talk to, he's already pulled out some bills from his pocket and paid for both of us.

"Let me pay you back," I say, reaching for my purse.

"My treat," he says firmly.

I wonder if we're on a date.

"What kind of music did you say they play?" I ask. He has to bend down low to hear me. He smells like soap and aftershave and something else, something spicy I can't name. The band must be taking a break, since there's a song I recognize from the radio blasting from the speakers.

"You'll love it," he says. Which doesn't answer my question, but it's really hard to talk. Someone bumps into me and I fly forward, crashing into Emmett. Maybe there's a real upside to going to a crowded club. He steadies me and I put my hands against his chest, pretending to get my bearings.

"Let's go up front," I say, and he nods in agreement.

We squeeze our way toward the stage, and by the time we get there, the band's back.

There's only three of them: a female lead singer with a guitar, a guy on drums, and another one standing by a small collection of instruments—two guitars, a bass, a trumpet and a few others I can't make out.

"Hey, everyone!" the female calls out. She has a smoky, velvety voice. Her face looks young, but her voice is old.

"We're from Seattle, Washington," she says, and someone in the back whoops. She tilts her head in acknowledgment. Someone else shouts out, "I like your shoes!"

"Thanks," she says. She's wearing bright purple boots over black tights and a black sleeveless dress. "Our van was broken into. We had a lot of serious equipment in there, and the only thing the thieves took was the bag with all my shoes. But they left this pair behind."

The crowd cheers and claps and laughs.

She gives a funny little bow and, with a nod of her head, the three of them begin to play. I can't help but move to the beat. Emmett was right, I love them. Playing a mix of edgy blues, folk and rock, they crank out song after song. The music has me moving and clapping and trying to remember the words.

After a long set, the whole room is pumped and full of energy.

"This place was built to sound good," she says, speaking into the mike once the crowd has settled down. "Do you mind if we try without this . . . ?" She waves to indicate the cords, the amps, the mike. The club has grown remarkably quiet as people listen to her. She steps away from the microphone. "Can you hear me in the back?" she asks without the amps. Her voice is quiet but clear.

"YEAH!" they roar back.

The other two guys, who must be brothers, unplug their instruments and step forward on either side of her, like an honor guard.

They both pick up guitars and begin to strum as she sings. The song is much quieter than anything else has been. The room grows still and silent; no one moves. It feels like the crowd is holding its breath, focusing on her. Her voice without the mike is clean and rich, soft as cashmere, pure as springwater. Everyone is watching her, but the thing is, the whole time she sings, she's looking straight at me.

"May Michael be at my right hand, Gabriel at my left; before me, Uriel; behind me, Raphael. And above my head, the Divine Presence."

I glance behind me, to my right and left, but there's no doubt it's me she's singing to. I tell myself she can't possibly know. She can't see through the bright stage lights; she's just focusing on a spot that happens to be where I'm standing. I try to keep from letting her song or her clear, lovely voice sneak into my soul.

Not you, I whisper in my heart. Don't be another angel, another messenger. I can't stand another one.

"It's okay," Emmett says to me. I hear his voice rumble and I turn in surprise. I hadn't realized I'd said anything out loud. He puts an arm around me and pulls me into him. "She's singing my favorite lullaby." That's when I realize that maybe she isn't singing to me. Maybe she's singing to Emmett.

I lean into his solid form, my stomach fluttering pleasantly at his warm chest, the hard knots of muscles. He smells spicy and earthy, like he'd walked through a cloud of incense.

The singer uses her voice like a velvet scalpel, softly cutting straight to the heart of the matter.

She finishes her lullaby, holding on to the last perfect note, and the room goes nuts. Wolf whistles, stomping, tribal whoops—after all that still, concentrated listening, the sudden release of energy is explosive.

"Glad you liked it," she says, smiling while the crowd worships her.

After another couple of sets and a wicked cover of "Sea of Love," the concert's over. It's past two, but I'm wired. We make it to the parking lot, among the last people out.

"It's late," Emmett says.

My ears are ringing in the aftermath of the concert. Except for the one acoustic song, the rest were played at top volume. I don't want to go home.

"Did you ever notice that you have two of each letter in your name?" I ask. I want to avoid the part where he says he should go, that this night is over. "You have two *e*'s, two *m*'s, two *t*'s. That's very balanced."

"If not for that pesky *a*, Miriam would be a perfect palindrome."

"Yeah, well, it's not."

He laughs. "You sound bitter."

"I've never liked my name."

"'Miriam the prophetess, the sister of Aaron,'" he intones. "'Took her drum in her hand and all the women went forth after her with drums and with dances.' Exodus 15:20."

It's late and we're standing under a cone of light from the streetlamp, the only ones out. To hear a biblical phrase here sounds almost sacred.

"You've memorized the Bible?" I'm trying to lighten the sudden tension, but I'm frightened. I'd forgotten my namesake was considered a prophetess. Is that what I am? Is that why the angels are coming to me?

"I remember bits and pieces," he says, answering my question. "I had a pretty traditional childhood."

He waits for the snarky comment, which he's left himself wide open for. With his shaved head and extensive tattoos, he's anything but traditional. But I don't feel like teasing him.

"My grandparents raised my sister and me after our mom died," he says after I don't jump in with a smart retort. "Dad left when I was five." He pauses, and I wonder if he doesn't tell many people that. I like to think that I'm special to him.

As special as he is to me. "My grandparents were good people," he says, as if remembering something. "Very religious and traditional. They would have liked you."

I'm beyond pleased by that compliment. I can't stop a shy smile.

I am hungry for these details. I want to know more about him, to know everything.

"Is your sister older or younger?"

"She's two years younger. She's a naval officer. Toughest person I know." His tone is both rueful and admiring. I wonder about their relationship: is it anything like mine and Mo's? As happens more and more when I think about Mo, I feel an aching twist in the pit of my stomach.

When I remain silent, he touches my shoulder.

"You okay?"

The night has fallen into that deep darkness that comes after midnight. It's cool outside, with a dampness that's settling on my skin.

"It's been a rough couple of days," I say. I try to think what else I can say to explain, but there aren't any words that would make sense. Not to anyone but me. Mo would understand, but I worry that he's slipping away from me. I worry that one day I'll call him and someone I don't know will answer. I push that thought away.

"You look . . ." He searches for the right word. "You look drained."

I exhale. Why do I think he was going to say "haunted"?

"You want a cup of tea or something?"

"I do," I say in great relief, so happy not to have to go home quite yet. "A cup of tea sounds perfect."

We drive off in his car, leaving the moment behind us like a bubble that will float up and away, without us.

He lives in a room above the tattoo parlor. When I finally see it, I'm disappointed. It isn't painted black with skulls, nor does his bed have rumpled red satin sheets or a studded leather comforter. There are bare wood floors swept clean, the old kind with wide honey-colored planks. The walls are a neutral off-white, and a ceiling fan turns slowly, barely stirring the air. His bed is made with tight hospital corners. The bedspread is the color of unbleached cotton. There's not much to the room. A table and chair, a lamp.

Emmett is downstairs fixing the tea, so I have time to take in the room. He's said I am free to look around, but there's nothing upstairs but this stark room and a bathroom down the short hall.

It could be anyone's room. A monk's, a soldier's, a student's. There isn't anything that marks his personality. Except that in a strange way, there is. Maybe it's the faint smell of his soap. Maybe it's the heavy black motorcycle boots standing so neatly near the closet. They weren't tossed there, they were placed there. There's an artist's pad of thick paper and several types of pencils in a jar. The desk faces a window to catch the light. I'm drawn to that closed notepad; I want to see what sorts of things he sketches when it's just for himself and not for a client with a story.

But I hear him coming up the stairs, so I pivot around with my back to the notepad. Other than the chair and the bed, there is no place to sit. Feeling awkward, I decide to lean against one of the walls.

"Make yourself at home," he says, only slightly ironic. He's holding two handle-less mugs that look like oversized Japanese teacups. He gives me one and I sip.

The hot tea slides down my throat, warming my stomach, soothing the roiling mess down there. It's fruity and minty and delicate, like a soft perfume.

"This is really good; what is it?"

"It's called A Thousand Winks. A friend of mine runs a tea shop in Florida. She sends me some."

"I like it."

It's quiet up here, though I can hear muted music coming from Mac's Irish Pub one street away. Just a bit of that fast, sharp beat, the occasional frantic melody of the fiddles. They'll be closing soon, it's that late. My mind is flitting around, trying to think about the concert, the singer. Trying not to think about Mo, about Tabitha, about God and angels, demons and the devil.

And then Emmett sets down his cup and stretches and I catch a glimpse of his stomach—tight, taut abs, seriously toned. Something simultaneously tightens in my chest and low down in my belly. The room feels warm. His neatly made bed with its pale cotton spread and dark wooden headboard suddenly seems to take up all the space in the room. My breath grows shallow and my heart rate kicks up.

Maybe I make a sound, because Emmett raises his head and turns to look at me. His black eyes are fierce, and I swallow.

"Miriam," he says, his voice deep and full. He sounds both amused and cautious. "What are you doing?"

That is a very good question. A better question would be, what am I thinking? But I'm not really thinking.

I step toward him. He takes a step back. His pants are snug, hugging his thighs and hips. I have to force myself to keep looking at his face. He's staring at me like I've pulled a grenade out of my purse.

"What, are you scared of me now?" I ask. The situation is almost funny, and strangely, it makes me feel better about my sudden desires. The room is thick with them.

He straightens at the barb and gives me a look. I stifle a laugh.

"It's okay," I say. "I don't bite." I set down my cup carefully. It's the pale lavender of early dawn, and the undulations of the cup suggest it's handmade. I wonder if this was a gift from his tea shop "friend." I wonder at the stab of jealousy I feel.

"Miriam," he answers with his usual bluntness. "You're young, and unless I'm mistaken, you're a virgin. I don't think either one of us is ready for a casual night."

His words do a lot to cool me down, but I can't stop myself. I'm not really thinking that far ahead. I'm not thinking about sex or commitments. I just want to touch him, very badly. To hold him and be held.

"Is that what this would be?" I ask him quietly.

"Miriam," he says, rubbing his shaved head. "Why are you

108

doing this?" The movement flexes his biceps and makes the tattoos roil.

I can't take my eyes off his arms. A dragon with green scales and a tail that curves around to the crook of his elbow. A palm tree (I think of the tea shop friend in Florida again). A snowcapped mountain, Fuji maybe. It's so sharp and clear I feel I should recognize it. Maori designs wrap around his wrists like shackles.

"What's the tattoo on your neck?" I ask him. I can only see a curving black shadow. The rest of it lies under his shirt. I have wondered about that tattoo.

"You're a beautiful girl," he says, and this time he reaches to touch my hair. "You should find a boy good enough for you."

"I just want to kiss you," I say softly, my heart hammering in my chest. "Just one kiss."

His hand plays with my hair as if he can't help himself, and I step a bit closer, though not so much as to spook him.

"Yesterday was my birthday. I'm nineteen, old enough to know what I'm doing." His sigh touches my face. "You don't have to do this," I say, feeling a fierce blush, a terrible humiliation, take hold.

His hands, large and sure, cup my face, the air heavy between us. He tilts my head and leans forward, and with our lips an inch apart, he stops. I can feel the heat from his face on mine. I want to surge forward, to close the distance, to attack his mouth and vent my frustration, my fear, my lust, my rabid fascination. Instead, I open my eyes, and as if that's the signal he was waiting for, Emmett closes the distance and we kiss.

He's soft at first. We touch lips, bumping together. He

slowly opens his mouth, his tongue slipping against mine. He's gentle, but I want more. I lean into him harder.

"All right, Miriam," he says against my ear. His breath and his words send shivers down my neck. "Okay."

His hands tighten, and he's kissing me as hard as I am him. His hands are in my hair, tilting my head for a better, deeper fit. He's holding on so tightly it skirts the edge of pain, almost scaring me. But I'm not scared, not really.

He steps back until he hits the bed and he sits down hard, as if he has lost his balance. But he doesn't let go of my face, so I'm pulled forward. To keep from falling, I drop my right knee on the bed, next to his hip. With one foot on the ground and one knee on the bed, I'm almost straddling him. The temperature in the room shoots up ten degrees.

His hands grasp my hips, thumbs right along my waistband.

He stops for a moment, as if to end it.

"No," I say, "not yet." And pull my other knee up on the bed, straddling him completely.

He adjusts his hands on my waist for a better grip as I sink down. He breaks contact long enough for me to haul his shirt up over his head. I feast my eyes on the designs revealed, natural and inked. I twist him around so I can see his back.

There, stretched out along the breadth of his back, spilling over his shoulder blades and curling up around his neck, is a giant angel, dark and fierce.

I freeze abruptly, my breath catching in my throat. Emmett's hands grow still as he senses something's wrong.

"Miriam?"

"Your angel," I say, reaching out to touch the sharply detailed feathers, then stopping myself a quarter inch from his skin. That's what's been peeking out of his shirt, curling around his neck—a feather from an angel's wings. It's been there this whole time. I shake myself, like a dog coming out of water. Oddly, a quote from Milton's *Paradise Lost* pops into my head, the last thing I read at college before I dropped out: *The mind is its own place, and in itself / Can make a heav'n of hell, a hell of heav'n*. The two have flipped so quickly, I can't tell where I am from one second to the next.

"Why did you get that done?" I ask. I feel like crying.

"I needed someone to watch my back," he says.

"Then you should have gotten a dog," I say. The words come out harshly. The mood is broken. I push back my hair, which is soft and tousled and probably a mess. I tug at my shirt. Nothing else has been disturbed. I tell myself that a great disaster has been avoided as I step away from the bed.

Emmett starts to say something, then stops.

"I should go," I say before this situation grows any worse. It is almost unbearably awkward. "I'm sorry." I wave a hand in his general direction. "I don't mean to be a tease."

Emmett takes my sudden change of heart with remarkable grace. There are no scowls, glares or insults. Instead, he looks worried. About me. He takes my hand in his large, warm palm and squeezes it gently, silently saying what words can't. Then he raises my hand to his mouth and presses a soft kiss in the moist center of my palm. I hug my hand to my chest, feeling my face flame red. He pulls on his shirt, and I'm sorry because

I haven't had a chance to see all his tattoos and because, damn it, I was close to having sex tonight. With Emmett. The thought still excites me.

"I—" How do I explain this? "I can't explain."

"Okay," he says.

My stomach is starting to cramp, and bitterly I realize I'll be spending much of tonight in the bathroom. Could this really be fixed with antibiotics? Suddenly I'm not at all certain the diagnosis is correct. I take a deep breath and focus on the current situation. On impulse, I lean forward and kiss a smooth-shaven cheek. Slowly, giving me a chance to bolt, he wraps his arms around me. With a quiet sigh, I lean a cheek against a hard, round shoulder, and we stay like that for a few minutes. Long enough for me to feel his heart beating steadily under the spot where our chests touch.

"Thank you for tonight," I say as I pull out of the world's best hug. "The concert, the tea . . . the kiss." What a euphemism. The most sensual, erotic ten minutes of my life is more like it. "You're a good friend."

"Anytime," he deadpans.

"Let me just use the bathroom before I go? Then I'll be out of your hair."

"I don't have any."

I smile at the weak joke. He points the way to the bathroom and I pray he'll be a gentleman and not stand too close to hear what's going on in there. Heading out, I catch a glimpse of our reflections in the window, the two of us looking thin and translucent against the black, dark night.

When I come out, he's downstairs, wearing a leather jacket and holding an extra one for me.

"What's this?"

"It's cold out," he says. "The car heater is broken."

I should say no. But I don't.

I climb in the passenger seat, slouching down, huddling in the cool warmth of his overlarge jacket. We fly through the quiet, sleeping streets. The ride barely lasts two minutes. He parks in front of my building. When I start to shrug out of the jacket, he stops me.

"Just bring it back to the shop," he says. "It's cold out tonight." We both realize he's created a reason for us to see each other again, and I'm grateful for it.

I nod my assent and then, with a last wave, head into my building, drained from the combined weight of disappointment, dull aching cramps and the now nearly familiar ache of feeling inadequate to the tasks ahead.

A line from the haftorah portion that I memorized for my bat mitzvah comes to me out of nowhere. A line I had forgotten about until now. *Heal me, O God, then shall I be healed; help me, then I shall be helped.* The prophet Jeremiah, using the old carrot and stick to inspire deeper devotion from the backsliding ancient Israelites. Guess I'm not the only slacker.

I don't know what God wants from me. I don't know if I can serve as He desires. And I wonder if He knows that. Maybe that's why it feels like everything is falling apart.

X.

WHEN I DON'T HEAR BACK from Dr. Kreger after a week, I call his office.

A bored receptionist puts me on hold, and shortly afterward the line goes dead. I call back, and this time I'm connected to a nurse.

"Miriam Abbot-Levy," I say, and then give her my birthday, my Social Security number and my address.

"Oh yes, here it is," she says finally. "You're all clear, sweetheart."

Her tone is so cheery and matter-of-fact that it takes me a second to register that this is bad news for me.

"Wait, what does that mean?" I ask, fighting a sudden wave of panic.

"No bacteria or parasites," she says, as if that's good news. I never thought I would ever wish to hear that I have worms.

"But that's what the doctor thought was wrong with me." I've been counting on a couple weeks' worth of antibiotics and no more diarrhea.

"Well, it's not," she says, her cheerful voice hardening into annoyance.

"So what am I supposed to do?"

"Sweetheart, that's something you need to talk with the doctor about."

I really, really hate it when strangers call me "sweetheart."

"Okay," I say. For some reason, I feel like crying. "Thanks."

"Sure. Bye, now." She hangs up. I call back and schedule a follow-up appointment.

I'm at work, in the middle of scanning a two-year-old wedding announcement, studying that unique, gushy style before I write my very first, when I'm suddenly lanced with a sharp, evil pain. It spears me right through my belly and I double over. It is so intense that I'm nauseous and my face turns clammy. I force myself to rise and hobble to the bathroom. I spend the next fifteen minutes cursing softly under my breath.

The next day I go to my appointment with Dr. Robert, the doctor Frank recommended. Back in yet another identical waiting room, I've already learned my lesson and bring a book to read. I can't keep my mind on it, though. I wonder if Frank's doctor will be any better. I try to be optimistic.

After sitting in the too cold room for only half an hour, I'm called in by a nurse. This time, when she tells me to strip, I say I prefer to keep my clothes on.

She pauses for a moment, hand on the doorknob, and

then shrugs as if I said something a bit eccentric but harmless. "Fine," she says. "Whatever."

My temper spikes at that, but at least I am not shivering and half naked.

The doctor knocks and enters soon after. Older and nicer than Dr. Kreger, he actually looks at me when I tell him about my symptoms. It's funny that Frank called him "a great young doc" since he's older than my father.

"And the stool test came back negative?" he asks after I've finished filling him in on what my current symptoms are, what the other doctor already covered and what he missed.

"Yes." I wait for him to tell me what's wrong.

"Then it's probably stress," he says.

"What?" I'm waiting for the punch line, for that twinkle in his eye that says he's kidding, indulging in a little medical humor before the big diagnosis.

"You've had a big move, a new job—you said there was a lot going on in your life."

"But I've been under stress before," I say, my voice rising. "I have never had anything like this happen. I have never even heard of anything like this happening to anyone."

"You would be amazed what stress can do to the human body," he says, not unkindly. "I advise you to take it easy. Get enough sleep, make sure you eat right, go for walks or get other forms of mild exercise. You're young and healthy; make sure you take care of your body, your mind, your soul, and you'll see everything will be right as rain." He pats my shoulder. "Any questions?"

I rub my face hard, like I'm trying to wake up.

"You're saying I have had diarrhea and horrible cramps, and have lost fifteen pounds in two months, because I'm stressed?"

"Exactly." He tsks, shaking his head. "You young people, you rush around too much. Stop 'texting,'" he says, using air quotes. "Take time to enjoy this beautiful earth that God gave you."

I stiffen at the mention of God. He sees that and, misunderstanding my reaction, he frowns slightly, then shuts my folder and stands up.

"If your symptoms continue for another month or worsen, come back and see me."

Before any words can pass the lump in my throat, he pats my shoulder again and leaves.

I sit on the examination table, trying to sort through my raging thoughts. I have been eating too many greasy fast-food meals, not enough sprouted grains and organic spinach, but then again, my diet is no worse than it has been for the past couple of years and maybe even a little better, considering the fresh produce I buy at the farmers' market.

I am getting a decent amount of sleep, and if anything is keeping me from sleeping enough, it's cramps and hot, achy joints. I have been living in terror of another visitation, of my own personal judgment day. Yet that's not going away anytime soon.

I scoot off the table and leave the clinic, but before I even make it out of the building, I have to turn around and use the bathroom. I hear two women come in, chat the whole time, then leave. I'm embarrassed, but also frightened. When I finally stand, the water in the toilet bowl has turned dark red. It reminds me of the first plague of Egypt: rivers turned to blood.

Shaky and weak in the aftermath of my very own plague, I decide that enough is enough.

A bacterial infection, I can understand. Stress? No. Freaking. Way.

As soon as I get home, I go online and start researching my symptoms. None of what comes up is good. All the possibilities, from cancer to bowel disease to major bodily disasters, require a specialist. So I look up gastroenterologists within a fifteen-mile radius. Seven names appear. I pick one in the middle with good reviews. When I call to make an appointment, the receptionist tells me the next available one is in six weeks. The thought of six more weeks of these cramps and frequent emergency trips to the bathroom pushes me close to tears. I manage to tell her no thanks before I hang up and try a different number.

One by one, I call them all, and the best I can do is to get an appointment with a Dr. Messa in two weeks. Perhaps because she hears the strain in my voice, the receptionist says she'll call if anyone cancels before that.

"Thank you," I say, genuinely touched by this act of kindness. "The sooner I can see him, the better."

I cancel my follow-up appointment at Dr. Kreger's.

But even assuming that Dr. Messa isn't callous or a moron, it's quite possible that whatever's plaguing me, like all of ancient Egypt's problems, has divine origins and is nothing any mortal doctor can fix.

I try to remember that warm feeling of love from the end of my dream. I try to hold on to those promises of safekeeping, that deep, impossible voice, those kind words. But a dream is a slippery thing, and I can't remember the exact words. Did the voice promise to protect me or to save me? Was there any mention of help? Healing? Even a vague mention of favor? My memory of the words is that they were lovely and kind, but I cannot glean any comfort from that. Fading fast, I'm left only with burdens and crosses to bear.

XI.

THOUGH HAMILTON IS SMALL, it has three locally owned coffee shops. My favorite is a small café tucked into an old factory built in the 1930s. The owners renovated the place but kept the original floor—thick-cut timber that darkened nearly to black from decades of wear. The café has high ceilings and sky-blue walls with chocolate-brown trim. Overstuffed chairs in faded velvet by large bay windows just beg for a body to curl up and tarry for a spell. Wi-Fi and lots of outlets mean I can get work done too.

I order a small tea and carry it to a chair by the window. The shop is unusually quiet for a Tuesday morning, and I'm more than pleased to snag such a prime spot. With my stomach a roiling mess, I've given up coffee. I keep hoping for something like the tea at Emmett's.

I pull out my notepad to plan my questions for Trudy at

the farm, where I have an appointment later this morning, but my mind keeps wandering and the pages fill with doodles. The rich-looking oil paintings in heavy gilded frames and the stamped metal plates on the ceiling lend the shop an old-world charm. I once asked the barista about the building, but she didn't know much except that it was "old." I wonder if tracking down the histories of the various buildings downtown would make a good story. I write a note to ask Frank.

I barely pay attention when the bell tinkles and a skinny teenager in baggy pants shuffles inside, probably skipping class. A muffled whoosh from the steamer and a clank from the espresso machine and the whole café fills with the smell of ground coffee and hot milk. I breathe it in, sigh with pleasure and then bury my nose in the mild, fruity scent of my tea, a pale imitation of the lovely infusion that Emmett had served me.

I expect the boy to pay for his drink and go, but after he takes a single sip, I hear him arguing with the barista. Something about his tone pulls me out of my reverie, and I look up from my notebook.

"I ordered a triple shot. This is watered-down crap."

"If you hate our coffee," she snarls, "why do you keep coming here?" The barista, with her multiple facial piercings, doesn't do customer service.

"I just want you to make it right. Okay? I'm paying four freakin' bucks for a cup of coffee. The least you can do is make it right."

"Fine." She sounds like she's grinding her teeth. "Hand it to me."

"Huh?"

"Give me your cup and I'll make you a new one."

His shoulders slump a bit and he reluctantly hands back the drink. I realize then that he'd hoped to keep the old "ruined" drink and score a second one for free. While the barista is knocking out old grounds with uncalled-for violence, the boy catches me looking at him and sneers. It comes across like a reflexive gesture. Nothing personal.

Within seconds, she's finished making his drink and hands it to him. He slurps a quick sip as she glares at him, daring him to complain again.

"It's okay," he mumbles. "It's better."

"Good."

Head down, hood back up, he shuffles out.

The barista watches him suspiciously until he's out the door and then glares at me too for good measure before disappearing through the curtain behind the bar.

I don't know what my face shows, but the hair on my arms is standing straight up and my stomach is cramping with sudden fear. As the boy was stalking out, I caught a glimpse of the badge we give to the high school interns at the paper. He's the new intern who started this week. But that's not what alarms me. As he was leaving, the morning sun shone through the glass door and I finally caught a good look at his face.

In my dream of Jacob's Ladder, I could make out three people being carried by angels. One was Tabitha, one was Mo and one was a complete stranger. I realize now that the sullen, surly ghostly image I saw was this intern's face.

I've just met my new mission.

* * *

A few hours later, my body weak, my composure in tatters, I keep my appointment with Trudy. I drive Frank's loaner to Sweetwater Farm. The countryside stretches out on either side of the road like a child's country play set: cows pastured on rolling green hills, horses that lazily look up as I pass. Occasionally I catch a glimpse of some impossibly huge estate tucked away at the end of a long, winding driveway, which reminds me that this is the home of country music and that this county, as Frank has told me more than once, is one of the richest in the nation.

I pull up to a small white clapboard house, and a dog comes running toward me, barking madly before I even turn off the ignition. The dog, a dirty, shaggy collie, barks and snarls outside the driver's side door, jumping up and scratching the paint. I stay in place.

"Samson! Stop it! Down, Samson!! Come here!"

Samson settles down a bit and looks mildly abashed. With one last halfhearted yip, he sinks back on all four feet, but doesn't budge from my door. I stay put.

The voice slowly grows closer and I make out Trudy in overalls and a baseball cap.

"Hey, beautiful," she says. "Glad you came. Hope Samson didn't scare you. He's a sweetheart." She reaches down and gives him an affectionate scratch behind the ears and a smack on the flank. "He just gets so excited when we have company."

With her there I feel brave enough to slowly open my door, my hand ready to pull it shut should Samson, the sweetheart, feel less than welcoming. But he sits there panting, tail whipping back and forth on the ground in a distinctly friendly wag that kicks up a small cloud of dust.

Once I'm out of the car, I stand still as Samson sniffs my hand and then jams a nose in my crotch.

"That's enough," says Trudy, pushing him away from me. "Come on inside. Let me get you something to drink and we can chat."

In town, the late spring heat is near stifling, but out here there's a nice breeze and something's blooming. I can't identify it, but as I follow Trudy into the house, memo pad and pen in hand, the scent relaxes a knot between my shoulder blades I wasn't even aware of.

It's much darker inside the house, and it takes my eyes a moment to adjust. I've dawdled so long at the door that Trudy's out of sight and I have to follow the sound of clinking glasses to find her in the kitchen.

She pours a couple of iced teas, and then I follow her to the back porch, a charming spot with pale blue paint peeling and cracking, wicker chairs with faded cushions and several wind chimes tinkling softly.

I open my notebook and scan my list of questions. "Are you ready to start?" I ask.

"Do your worst."

"Okay, um, so what inspired you to be a farmer?"

"Now, that's an interesting question," she says. I try not to wince. Good, intriguing questions are the cornerstone of a good, intriguing article. "Interesting," as my father explained once, is not a positive adjective. It's neutral at best, and probably simply means "bad." It means the person can't think of

124

anything else to say. A great way to start things off. "I guess I've always been fascinated by growing things. Even as a child I had a little pizza garden: I grew tomatoes, basil, oregano and onions."

"That's so cute," I say, scrambling to write down her comments.

"I never really thought about farming professionally, though. I went to college, worked for the CIA."

I stop writing and stare at her in surprise.

She laughs at my expression. "Now, why does that always seem to shock folks?"

"What did you do for the CIA?" I ask. I'm going off the list, but this tangent is worth following.

"Nothing too exciting. I was a data analyst. Spent a lot of time in Washington, got to see a bit of the world."

I make a face at her vagueness.

"Sorry, beautiful," she says. "There really aren't any skeletons in the closet." She makes a face. "At least no *interesting* ones."

"So, what makes a CIA spook decide to be a crunchy-granola, tree-hugging farmer?"

She laughs, liking my sarcastic tone better than the oh-so-serious proper journalistic one. "I got sick of bureaucrats—the constant power struggles, the petty rivalries; the stress, the smog. Everything got to me. I took a leave of absence to put my head back on straight. I knew I couldn't keep working for the government, but I sure didn't know what I could do.

"I was traveling around, visiting old friends I'd barely kept in touch with over the years, when I came here, met Hank."

She takes a pause to drink her tea. I'm too busy writing to do the same. But she waits in silence until I finish and then says, "Go on, drink a bit before we continue."

I do. The tea is oversteeped, a very sweet, classic southern iced tea, perfect on this unusually hot day. The breeze has died down, and even in the shade, I feel moisture bead on my forehead and upper lip. I rest the cold, sweating glass on my face briefly before setting it down.

"Here I am, all pale and flabby from fifteen years of cubicle life, and there's Hank, seven years my senior, tanned and strong, with so much pride about what he's doing in this world. All the good he's doing. He was farming organically way before it became the new yuppie crusade. It's a beautiful thing to see the land thrive, to see birds and butterflies returning with the seasons, to get to know your customers. Knowing that you're helping them.

"So one thing leads to another, and instead of keeping on with my road trip, I decided to stay here for a while to see what I thought of it." She spreads her arms out to encompass herself, the porch, the fields. "I'm still here. But by now I've discovered that besides all the poetic sunshine I just fed you, farming is also backbreaking work, it's something you can't really take a vacation from, because the farm always needs tending and the weeds and the deer don't really care about your calluses or that shopping trip to the store you've been putting off or that little getaway to Italy you've been dreaming about. It also hardly pays enough to keep the roof over our heads. But as the old cliché goes, my worst day at the farm beats the hell out of my best day in Washington.

"When I lived in Tibet—"

I break a cardinal rule of interviewing and interrupt her. "You lived in Tibet?"

She ignores me.

"—what impressed me was their closeness to the land. The seasons passing, the harsh weather: they didn't shelter themselves from it, they embraced it. That's kind of what I'm trying to do. Embrace what it means to feed people. To tend to the land. It feels downright biblical sometimes."

"Especially the part about the ten plagues," a deep voice rumbles to my right.

I turn to see Hank coming out, mopping his face with an old, faded bandanna and holding his own glass of dark sun-brewed tea.

"You're feeding this girl more hippie dogma than folks at a macramé convention."

"Can I quote you on that?" I ask with a laugh.

He doesn't mind, but Trudy says no.

With a poorly suppressed groan, he sits down next to Trudy on the musty, worn velvet settee. The porch furniture is a mishmash of outdoor wicker furniture, only slightly peeling and dusty, and several old-fashioned indoor pieces in odd fabrics like purple velvet. It's what shabby chic looked like before it was chic.

We chat for a while, the conversation flowing nicely as Hank and Trudy walk me though a typical farm day. It sounds impossibly difficult, but from their easy banter and light-hearted manner, it's obvious that they love it. As they talk, it becomes clear they both came to agriculture by accident.

Neither was a farm-bred kid. The closest Hank ever got to a farm was a fifth-grade trip to a dairy farm.

Hank had been a college professor for years at a small liberal arts school in Vermont, teaching philosophy and religion. He still teaches an occasional class at the local community college.

"You know my students go online to find out the weather? 'It's gonna rain,' they tell me when it's already raining outside." He's trying to be funny, but his voice grows agitated, losing some of its calm cadences. "A big part of the reason we're in the sorry shape we're in is because most people are so insulated from what happens to growing things when it rains too much, or not at all."

Trudy glances over at him and eventually puts her hand over his. As if that's his cue, he takes a deep breath, then shrugs ruefully.

"You've found my hot spot," he says to me.

"I think you've scared her off," Trudy scolds him. "Come on, beautiful, let's take a break from all this jabbering and give you a quick tour of the place, all right?"

The farm is not as large as I imagined. For it to produce the amount of crop sold at the market, I'd pictured rolling hills with rows and rows of seedlings, beans, herbs. But instead, they tell me that the farm is only fifteen acres, of which only ten are actively producing crops. Ten acres would be a very large backyard. But it makes for a rather small farm. Though when they explain how much weeding, watering, fertilizing and harvesting there is to do, the farm begins to loom large again.

Volunteers who want to learn about organic farming come and go. They stay for a couple of months, sleeping on the porch or in tents, eating their meals with Hank and Trudy. I meet two of them. Nearly androgynous, with the same creamy white skin and thick, grimy dreadlocks, they smile peacefully at me, reminding me of statues of the Buddha, though they are thin to the point of gauntness. I try to coax a few quotes from them, but they don't say anything that will look good on paper.

Thinking about how I'm going to put everything I've learned into a meaningful article helps push away all the serious things I should be thinking about. But always, that niggling kernel of unease, that line of tension and fear running down my spine, is there. And now that I've seen my new mission, I'm pulled in twin directions: hope that my chance for redemption is here; fear that once again I'll fail.

Trudy and Hank point out various planting tactics they've learned that naturally help protect their crops. Marigolds near lettuce, roses near grapes. On the other hand, you can't plant garlic or onion near strawberry plants, since the fruit will pick up some of the pungency.

"We heard that deer hate Irish Clean—you know, the soap. We bought cases of the stuff and strung it up all over the lettuce. Middle of the night, I hear something." Trudy pauses dramatically. "I creep up in the darkness . . . and find a deer licking the bar between nibbles of the lettuce."

I laugh.

"We ended up giving away soap with that week's share," Trudy says.

After the half-hour tour, we head back to the house. Trudy and Hank urge me to stay for lunch and I do.

"You've lost some weight since you've moved here," Trudy mentions as she sets plates down on the long farmhouse table. The interns will be joining us.

I shrug. It's the one silver lining to this stupid thing I'm going through: my weight is sort of fading, just coming off without any intent on my part. It's kind of nice. Though even I have to admit dropping weight because my insides are liquefying is probably not healthy.

"You've got to take care of your body," Trudy scolds over her shoulder as she reaches for a serving bowl. "You young kids don't realize how precious a strong, healthy body is. Take it from me," she says, placing the bowl on the table and rubbing her lower back. "You miss it when it's gone."

"Yeah," I say dryly. "I believe you."

After lunch, Trudy has to check on the seedlings the interns planted. She gives me a tight hug and kisses my cheek, surprising me. I've thought of a couple more questions, so Hank and I chat in their office. As charming and shabby as the rest of the house, the office consists of a large, messy desk, two chairs, some stunningly beautiful landscape paintings—I recognize the view from the house looking out to the fields—and cheap bookcases, their shelves bent under the weight of books.

Hank tells me a bit more about his plans for the future of the farm, his theories on organic farming. But after a while, I lose my concentration. My stomach suddenly starts cramping. I feel a cold sweat break out as I struggle to contain the waves of pain rolling through my gut.

"Deliver us from sickness," Hank says, his deep voice rumbling prophetically through the small, book-lined office.

"What?" I ask, jolted.

"It's the most common graffiti found at ancient holy sites," he says, removing his pipe from his mouth and frowning at something in the bowl. "Not requests for riches, not personal glory, not sexual boasting. Just health." I have no idea why he's drifted to this topic. But since he's a teacher, I guess he's used to lecturing. "We tend to discount the preciousness of health—until we lose it, of course. Since we rarely lose it in this day and age, we don't think much of it. We rely on science, on medicine, to fix what's broken. But the fact is, even today, in our great modern civilization, so much sickness is inexplicable. Random." He makes a vague motion with his pipe, like a conductor with a baton. "Unfixable."

I shift uncomfortably.

"So ill health is divine punishment?" I say hesitantly. I don't even want to articulate this, but something propels me.

"Ah," he says, a pleased professor drawing out discussion in class. "Illness in the ancient world was so common, so mysterious. Even as recently as the nineteenth century, most letters begin with the writer assuring the recipient of his good health and expressing his concern about the health of everyone back home. Men in their prime died after a small cut, after contracting a mild cold. Healthy children died within days of coming down with diarrhea. Who else could be powerful enough? The devil or God, take your pick."

I shiver at his words, hugging myself almost unconsciously.

"Horrible," Trudy says, walking in the office.

"Yes, sickness and death were very much a part of everyday life. Many believed sickness came from the devil. How else to explain it?"

Trudy sits on the arm of Hank's chair and rubs his neck and shoulders.

"What about God?" I ask. "Couldn't illness be punishment? Or inflicted because it suits His purpose?"

"Certainly. The Judeo-Christian God seems perfectly capable of this. There's Job and his boils. Then, of course, there's the flip side of it: Jesus curing the lepers." He frowns at his pipe, then puts it in his mouth and draws deeply, releasing a strong but pleasant scent along with a small puff of smoke. Then he looks back at me, pale blue eyes sharp and steady. "The devil might cause illness, but ultimately it's all in God's control, isn't it? To mete out sickness or relieve it, it's His choice."

My thoughts flit back to the morning's encounter with the coffee scammer.

"How do you get God to help you instead of hurt you?" I ask.

"Now, there's a question." Hank puffs again on the pipe as he ponders what must seem like a nice rhetorical question. "People have been trying to answer that one for as long as there's been misfortune. Some would say prayer; some religions believe in offerings or sacrifices. There's always charity, good deeds." He pulls on his beard. "But I believe things happen for a reason. And if God wants something, even something bad, to happen, there's nothing little old you can do to change His mind."

I look down at my hands.

"That's pretty cold," I finally say.

"At our church we pray to a benevolent God," Trudy says, her tone gentle. "And I believe that He is good and kind. But I also think that we can't know what He has planned for us. It's often not what we would wish."

I appreciate her attempts to ease the sudden dark atmosphere. This whole area of Tennessee is rather obsessed with church attendance. There are more churches than restaurants here, and on Sundays there are massive traffic jams around the megachurches. It seems so fake to me, more of a social event than a spiritual one, but Trudy and Hank seem so calm and grounded. Since farmwork isn't nearly as lovely and peaceful as it sounds, I'm curious where they find that inner peace.

"What church do you go to?" I ask, pulling out my reporter's notebook.

"First Baptist. It's a wonderful place; you should come with us on Sunday."

"Oh, thank you. But I'm Jewish. . . ." Sort of, kind of.

"Ah," she says. "I hope I haven't offended you."

"No, of course not."

"Have you found a synagogue to go to?" she asks. I could swear that Hank is trying to kick her under the table.

"No. I'm not . . . I haven't been very observant, so I might look for one, but for now . . ." I trail off, figuring I should stop blabbing. Trudy looks at me with something close to pity, like I'm a lost little puppy and she wishes she could take me home.

"Judaism is one of the most cerebral religions," Hank says.

He stops fiddling with his pipe and meets my eyes. "It's always such a pleasure to read a rabbinical Bible interpretation."

"I've taken enough of your time," I say. "I know how busy you are." I rise and shake their hands. "Thanks for lunch; the article should be out in the next couple of weeks."

"Come back anytime," Trudy says kindly.

I know Mo would laugh at me. But I feel like maybe Hank and Trudy already know what's going on.

I head to the newsroom to start putting together my article on Sweetwater Farm. As I'm transcribing quotes and getting down all my impressions, I'm also keeping an eye out for my young hoodlum, the new intern whose name I don't know yet. The few people around the newsroom just shrug when I ask them about the high schooler. This guy, this bad-tempered, surly loser, is precious and special or he wouldn't have been singled out. He's also my mission, and I can't lose sight of what's really important this time. I'm not clear what I'm supposed to protect him from, but there's no freaking way I'm letting him get hurt.

Frank is out for the day, so I can't grill him about the new intern.

Around four-thirty, I see a slouching, shuffling form slink by. I pop up from my chair and hurry after it.

"Hi!" I call out. But the intern doesn't turn around. I call out, a little louder, "Hi! You there, hi!" But he keeps on walking. I suddenly catch a glimpse of telltale white wires and earbuds. He's listening to his iPod. With a final burst of speed, I grab a handful of his oversized hoodie. He spins around, eyes blazing at the touch.

I quickly release him and step back.

"Hi," I say again.

He just stands there and stares at me, not removing his earbuds.

"I'm Miriam," I say, offering my hand. "I work here?"

With insulting slowness he gives me a limp hand to hold. I can hear the music spilling out of the earbuds, a tinny beat that must be blasting inside his skull. He probably can't even hear me, only see my lips moving.

"I just wanted to introduce myself, see if you had any questions?" I wait for him to turn off, or at least turn down, the music. But he just stands there. So I keep talking. "Anything you were really hoping to get to do while you're here for your internship?"

He shrugs. I try for a direct question that needs an answer.

"What's your name?"

"Jason," he says. I'm surprised he can actually hear me.

"Well, hi, Jason. I'm Miriam—well, I guess I already said that. But anyways . . ." I'm trying way too hard to break through his complete opaqueness and probably coming across like a spaz. "Nice to meet you, Jason. I hope you like it here as much as I do."

After another moment of mutual staring, I turn and head back to my desk, kicking myself for the lame introduction and plotting how to better get to know him. Jason is no Tabitha.

I feel like I've been bumped up to level II of difficulty

without ever mastering level I. I don't have a clear mission or even an easy subject to get to know. Not only do I need to figure out what to save him from, I need to break through to him in order to do that.

After finishing my notes, I put my story on hold for the rest of the day, focusing only on how to appeal to Jason. I'm so clearly not the kind of person he cares for—not cool enough, not tough. I think of Emmett. Emmett is cool. I haven't seen him since the night after my birthday. I still have his jacket, folded on a chair in my bedroom. I like looking at it, and I haven't had the nerve to go back to his shop. Maybe it's time I found the courage.

I'm full of plans as I leave for the day.

I wonder if I can tell Jason that God is watching him. That I was charged with turning his life around, with keeping him safe. But something in me is convinced I'm not supposed to do that. I stifle the impulse to tell him about my dream. It's not like Jason would believe me anyway.

That night, I'm sick again: bad cramps, chills and a hot ache in my knees and elbows. Is this my punishment, the whip to spur me on?

"Please," I say out loud in my darkened room, huddling in my disheveled bed. If there's anything there watching me, I can't feel it. "I'm on the case. I've met Jason. I am doing my best."

But of course there's no response. No sign that anyone has heard me, or if they did, nothing to show that anyone cares.

XII.

FIRST THING IN THE MORNING, I have my appointment with Dr. Messa, the gastroenterologist who agreed to see me the soonest.

The waiting room is full of old people half slumped over in their chairs. I'm the only one here under fifty. I have to bite my lip to keep from humming the *Sesame Street* song: *One of these things is not like the others.* An hour-long wait and I'm prepared for another blow-off. But after the doctor sees me, he's very concerned.

"We need to look at what's going on."

Look? I think.

"I want to schedule you for a scope as soon as possible. On your way out, talk with Megan and she'll see what we can do."

Scope?

He notices my expression.

"We'll do a colonoscopy. Are you familiar with the term?"

"Aren't I too young for that?"

He smiles. "We recommend a routine colonoscopy for everyone over fifty, but that's for colon cancer screening. In your case, we need to see what's causing all this distress. We insert a very small camera that can look at your entire colon to give us a better sense of what's going on in there."

My eyes grow round as I picture what he's saying.

"But what do you think it could be?" I ask, my voice so small I can barely recognize it. A camera . . . up there??

"Frankly, you're presenting classic signs of irritable bowel disease—that is, Crohn's—or ulcerative colitis. I won't know which until your colonoscopy. Since we've ruled out a bacterial infection, unfortunately it's the most likely scenario, given your age."

"What does that mean?" I whisper.

"There are some helpful pamphlets on your way out that you should read. But we really need to see what the scope reveals before we go borrowing trouble. Have you ever had a colonoscopy before?"

I shake my head mutely. Miserably.

He softens a bit at my expression.

"It's not nearly as terrible as you might think." He pats my hand. "The most unpleasant part is the prep."

"The prep?" I'm only echoing what he says; none of this is sinking in.

"You have to clear out your colon before I can see anything with the scope. You'll need to drink a special solution. . . . I believe it's been described as a 'tidal wave,'" he says dryly.

I swallow with difficulty.

"But you'll get through that, and then we'll see what we're dealing with, okay?" He rises. "Make sure you speak with Megan on your way out."

It takes me a few minutes before I gather myself enough to leave the room. I wanted to ask: *Are you sure it isn't stress? I prefer salmonella; can't we just stick with that?* But deep down, I know that there's more wrong with me, and so I leave the exam room, pick up a pamphlet and schedule my first-ever colonoscopy for next week, about thirty-one years earlier than usually recommended.

I call Frank and tell him I won't be coming in that day. He's not real happy about it and grumbles about needing to pull my own weight. Normally something like that would upset me no end. But today I just say, "Sure, I'll try harder next week," and hang up on him.

As I head up the staircase to my apartment, I think about the colonoscopy. I also think about Jason and what I could possibly do for him. If I do help him, is there any way this mess would fix itself before next week's procedure? I'm not paying attention to much except my thoughts, and so I nearly trip over a large duffle bag in the hall almost blocking the way to my apartment.

"What the—" I start to curse.

I hear a familiar laugh and snap my head up.

There he is, lounging against the doorjamb.

"Hey, sis," Mo says, spreading his arms out wide. "Guess who's come over for a visit?"

XIII.

Mo doesn't answer questions he doesn't like, and so, despite my prodding and poking, he doesn't give me a good answer for why he's here. Yes, finals are over. Yes, summer jobs are hard to find. He missed me, and aren't I glad he's here?

I feel ashamed that my first reaction to seeing him at my door is suspicious mistrust. My own brother. I *am* glad to see him. Mo has a way of charging the atmosphere. Everything is funnier, crazier, wilder when he's around. On impulse, I grab him and hug him. Instinctively he hugs me back, a tight, hard hug that feels great. But then he lets go and skitters sideways, almost dancing away from me. He asks more questions than I do, taking charge like usual. So I still don't know why he's here, or for how long. I don't think the visit is permanent, because there really isn't much room in the apartment, and I don't see him finding a job here in Hamilton, but he's brought enough with him to last the summer.

"Things will work out," he says blithely, brushing aside my concerns. I keep thinking about having to share a bathroom. Even if it's with my own brother, what I have going on is nothing I want to share. "The couch is fine with me. I won't crash here for long. You'll just have to tell all those guys you're shacking up with, all those one-night stands, to wait a bit till I'm gone."

I roll my eyes.

"Like I don't know you've slept with half the city."

I punch him in the shoulder. It's an old tease of his, my promiscuity. Kind of like calling a bald man Curly.

In the end, there's nothing I can do. There was never any question of whether I'd let him stay. Of course I would, of course. It's Mo. I watch as he heads into the kitchen, opens the fridge and helps himself to a pitcher of iced tea.

Maybe he's just the thing I need. If there's anything Mo's good at, it's distraction. And maybe I'm just the thing he needs too. With him close to me, how much trouble can he get into?

Mo talks me into going with him to the park. He's brought lunch, and we sit on a picnic table, feet resting on the bench, and eat fried chicken legs.

"This stuff is so gross," I say, wiping endless quantities of orange grease from my fingers and shredding the thin napkins in the process. According to a Web site I found, I'm not supposed to eat fried food. No spicy food. And easy on the roughage. But I eat the chicken anyway, cramps be damned. Literally.

"What?" he says through a mouthful of chicken. "These are great."

I hold up three used, grease-stained napkins. "Exhibit A."

"This is the best damn fried chicken in the state, sis. An old man down at the gas station told me where to buy it. I don't think you appreciate how lucky, yes, lucky, you are to enjoy this—might I add free—lunch."

He's on his pulpit. I let him ramble and my thoughts wander away.

The good thing is that Mo doesn't need or insist on full attention when he steps into his preachy mood; simple presence is enough. So I watch the little kids on the playground and the bigger kids playing touch football on the grass.

Like much in Hamilton, Greenbrier Park is perfect. The perfect city park. There's a half-mile gravel path for the power walkers and joggers, and there are two playgrounds, one for the preschool set and one for the elementary school kids. A wide, grassy field is kept religiously mowed so that dandelions barely have a chance to pop their yellow heads up before being whacked off in the name of perfect order.

No basketball courts with rattling metal nets here. No baseball diamond with a rusty chain-link fence. Just the wholesome goodness of a grassy field that your imagination can turn into anything it wants.

Greenbrier Park is so orderly, so perfectly planned, that it should feel artificial and cloying. But it doesn't. It's like

Mayberry come to life. Even knowing about the ruins that lie two miles into the woods from here, I like it.

Mo is winding down, so I turn to him and make a few "mm-hmm" sounds to keep him happy.

Our picnic table is near the preschool playground. A heavy woman wearing a floppy straw hat with a giant plastic sunflower pinning up the brim hovers over a fat three-year-old girl. The woman crouches at the foot of the slide, her arms outstretched like she's ready to corral a runaway calf. The little girl slides down with no problem and then clambers off, waddling toward the ladder to start again. The mom helps her up the rungs even though the girl seems perfectly capable and is rather annoyed with her mother. Sweaty and wearing a pink shirt that declares I'M A LITTLE PRINCESS, she scowls as her mother flutters here and there, calling out, "Be careful, sweetie. Let Mommy help you, Emily Elizabeth."

"Jesus," Mo says, sotto voce. The "Greatness of Fried Chicken" sermon has ended. "I think that freaking toddler weights as much as I do."

"Snack time, Emily Elizabeth. Mommy brought all sorts of yummies."

"Deep-fried in lard, every one," he mutters in my ear.

I have to stifle a giggle, though his joke is rich, coming from Mr. Fried Chicken Lover. The toddler's fat cheeks hang low like jowls, and her shirt strains against her tummy. While I understand that little girls love pink, on Emily Elizabeth's round body the shirt, combined with her currently bright red face, makes her look astonishingly like a plump little piglet.

As the mom turns to adjust the large gingham diaper bag on her shoulder, her eagle eyes not looking for just a moment, Emily Elizabeth steps back, away from the top of the slide, and her little foot slips.

"Oh," I gasp. Disaster is imminent. I stand and half lunge toward the scene as it unfolds. The mom's head snaps up and turns to her girl at the sound of my gasp.

"Emily Elizabeth!" she cries, diving forward, but it's too late. The girl's thick plastic shoes slip off the narrow metal rung and she falls, hitting her chin on the ladder hard enough to make her head jerk back as she plummets the rest of the way. She lands with a heavy thud and lies terrifyingly still in a crumpled heap before starting to shriek in a piercing wail. The mom drops to her knees and holds her daughter, rocking her and fighting her own tears.

"Baby, let me see the side of your head," she pleads, but the girl won't let her.

The mom seems near panic, and maybe a cool though medically untrained head might help.

"She smacked her chin," I say, coming over and crouching near the pair. "It'll probably grow into a big knot, but she should be okay." I speak in what I hope is a calm, soothing tone.

The mom looks at me for a second before turning her attention back to her girl. "She has a—" but I don't catch the word. The mom continues, "It means she has a shunt in the side of her head. It drains excess spinal fluid. I don't think she hit it, but you know . . ."

I suddenly feel like an idiot with my platitudes.

"Oh." I reassess the toddler, who's stopped crying by now

and is sniffling into her mom's comfortable bosom. "Do you want me to call 911?"

I hear Mo cough decisively, but then he hasn't heard what the woman said over the wails of her daughter.

"No, she's fine. This is her first major fall, is all. I've got two other kids, boys. They were barely one before they had a big old goose egg or shiner, and she's three." The woman strokes the damp curls softly. "I know I can't keep her in a bubble, but I can't help trying anyhow." She caresses the girl's forehead in a gesture that is as automatic as it is loving.

"You're a good mom," I say gently. "She's lucky to have you."

Emily Elizabeth—who I now see has beautiful blue eyes, brilliant against her reddened skin—looks up at me. She starts sucking her thumb.

"Thank you," the mom says. "Some days I really need to hear that."

"Are you sure you don't need me to get you anything?"

"We're fine," she says, patting her daughter's back. "We'll be just fine."

I rise and walk over to where Mo, who's given up on me, has joined an impromptu game of soccer. He kicks the ball around for a bit and then returns.

"Miriam, how in the hell do you find patience for all the wackos out there?"

"She's not as bad as she seemed. She had a really interesting story."

"You're a soft touch, Miriam Abbot-Levy," he says, grinding a knuckle into my hair.

"Ouch, stop that!"

"I'm bigger and older."

"By three inches and five minutes!"

He grins at our old taunts.

"Bet you can't catch me," I say.

"Betcha I can."

I take off, dodging soccer players, playground equipment and a couple of trees. He only lets me get away for a few minutes before he decides the fun's over. I don't even see him coming, just feel the impact as he tackles me. We fall down on the grass in a heap of legs and arms. My knees scrape the ground and my elbow hits a small rock with a painful jolt.

"Bastard," I say, looking up at the clouds and the sky.

"What does that make you, then?"

"Bastard's twin sister."

He laughs, and I join in. We lie side by side, watching large, fluffy clouds drift by. Mo reaches for my hand and squeezes it.

"I missed you," he says.

I squeeze his hand back. This is my chance to ask him why he came. I've had a second encounter; perhaps he did too. At any rate, he's definitely keeping something from me. But if he hasn't had a visit, he'd be hurt and insulted that I assumed it was the only reason he came to see me. As I waffle, trying to find a tactful way to bring the topic up, Mo lets go of my hand and stretches.

"Come on, Florence Nightingale," he says, pulling me up to my feet. "Let's go see what else this center of culture and learning has to offer."

Later, while we're eating dinner in front of the TV, it strikes me why the little girl's name was so familiar.

"Clifford!" I exclaim right as a car on the screen flips during a high-speed chase.

"What?" Mo says, irritated at the interruption.

"Emily Elizabeth is the little girl from the Clifford books—you know, the big red dog."

"I loved those books," Mo says, giving me his attention now that the car chase has ended. "I always wished I had such a big dog to ride around on. I'd sic him on all the mean kids in the neighborhood. We'd rule the world."

I ignore these delusions of grandeur. "Do you remember how Clifford got so big?"

"He was a freak?"

"No." I punch him. "Emily Elizabeth was worried because Clifford was the runt of the litter. Her love made him grow."

Mo howls with laughter and ends up almost choking on pepper steak. I slap him on the back, a little too helpfully. "That is freakin' hilarious," he says. "That fat-cow mom was really asking for it, wasn't she?"

"She's not that bad."

"Come on, Miriam, you saw how she was dressed, how she was pushing food on her fat daughter—one cow raising another."

"Her daughter has medical issues!"

"Sure. Let me guess. 'Slow metabolism'?"

"Mo, she told me—"

He shushes me. "This is where he blows this guy's face away; you've got to see this." He turns up the volume and my living room is filled with a series of loud pops and the wet sound of bullets hitting flesh. I stop trying to tell him anything and focus on forcing down a few bites of white rice.

When we clear up the mess and make the couch into a bed later that night, he notices my almost untouched order of Buddha's Delight.

"Don't go all anorexic on me, sis," he says. "You've lost a few pounds. You look good. Quit while you're ahead."

"Bugger off," I say in Mom's best British accent.

He waggles his fingers and winks, and I leave for my bedroom. I close the door behind me and press a hand to my roiling guts. "Bugger you too," I say to them.

I'm scared of the colonoscopy. But I'm ready for something to end this already. As I lie in bed, I try different relaxation techniques to help me fall asleep. Visualization of favorite places. Deep breathing. Repetitive mantras. But in the end, there's only one thing that helps me relax and turn off the continuous loop of Jason, colonoscopy, pain, God, Raphael, angels, failure. As I do sometimes, I picture Emmett: his shaved head, his deep-set dark eyes, the brilliant colors of the tattoos covering his arms. And I pretend that he's here. Sometimes I imagine that instead of his black leather jacket folded on the corner chair, it's him sitting there, watching over me. Sometimes I'm more daring.

Like tonight.

Tonight Emmett is in bed with me. He's got his heavy arms wrapped around me, pressing me up against his strong, broad chest. My ear is resting on his warm, solid torso as his heart beats a slow, steady beat. Since I'm trying to get to sleep, not get all excited, all we do is snuggle together. He's radiating heat like an oven. He lets me tuck my cold feet between his calves.

I hear Mo in the living room. He turns the TV up and then heads to the kitchen. Cabinets open, close; glasses and dishes clink.

But I ignore that and focus on Emmett. He murmurs that it's late, that I need to sleep. He promises to keep an eye on things. I pretend that his heart is thumping gently next to me, and it calms me so that eventually my own heart settles into a similarly calm cadence.

I curl on my side, hugging a pillow, and drift off to sleep.

I sleep fitfully—first I'm hot, then cold, waking up chilled or in a sweat. The covers tangle around me and I can't settle down. My dreams are restless, uncomfortable. I wake up for what must be the fifth time of the night and nearly shriek in fright.

It takes my sluggish brain a second to realize the dark shape of a man in the corner is Mo. Headlights from a passing car momentarily illuminate the room and catch the whites of his eyes, lighting them silver.

"You scared me," I say, pressing a hand to my chest, as if to still my leaping heart. My hands are shaking from the adrenaline rush and I feel slightly nauseous.

"Sorry," he says, his voice low and quiet. As if there is someone left to be careful of, as if there is someone still sleeping.

"Are you okay?" How long had he been there, watching me sleep?

"I'm fine," he says, not moving from his low slouch in the chair. "Go back to sleep, everything's fine."

"Mo," I say, pushing away sleep-crazy hair, trying to see his features in the dim room. "What's going on? Why are you sitting there?"

"I had a bad dream," he says. "I wanted to make sure you were okay. I wanted to make sure you were breathing."

When we were little, we used to have nightmares about each other. And when we woke up, we'd creep into the other's bed to make sure everything was okay, that he and I were still alive.

"You're too old to come into bed with me," I say, profoundly uneasy. For some reason, my heart rate kicks back up. "It was just a bad dream."

"I know." He sounds so sad. "I know."

"Go back to sleep," I insist. "It's late."

He sits there for a moment longer, so still that I'm not sure he's breathing. Then, with a sigh, he rises slowly. Something about the way he's holding himself, so carefully, worries me.

"Are you okay?" I ask again.

He doesn't answer.

Then, in the dark, sleep-heavy room, I ask what I've been scared to ask all day. "Mo," I say softly. "Did he come back? Does he want more from you?" I don't say the name. I'm scared to at night. I'm scared to when Mo is acting so strangely.

But he doesn't answer, shuffling out of my bedroom as if he's sapped of all his strength, like someone at the end of his rope.

I'm wide-awake now and worried, though not about

myself this time. It doesn't add up—this visit from Mo, his odd behavior. Maybe he didn't hear my question. Maybe he doesn't want to answer. I fret in bed, annoyed by the hot pillow, the smothering blankets, my aching joints. I try to pretend Emmett is here, but this time the image doesn't come. Maybe he's confused by all this too.

No sounds come from the living room. I wonder if Mo fell back asleep or if he's lying on the couch, staring at the ceiling like me.

With Mo, you have to give him the space to come to you on his own. He knows I care, that I love him. That must be why he's here in my apartment in the first place. He needs my help.

Decision reached, I feel a warm peace slip its way into my chest and glide down, warming and relaxing all my limbs. I quickly fall asleep.

XIV.

IN THE MORNING, I wonder if I dreamt the whole encounter. Mo is jumpy with excess energy, pulling my hair, pinching my arm and dancing away from my flung-out smacks.

"Did you sleep okay?" I ask.

"Like the dead." His eyes roll to the back of his head and he makes a horrid face at me, tongue hanging out. Then he turns to fix a bowl of cereal.

It's hard to talk to him when he's in this mood, and with his back to me, I can't tell what he's thinking. But I try again. "I mean, after we talked, you slept okay?"

As if he has read my mind, he turns to me and rolls his eyes, face slack. There's no point asking him anything right now.

He barely eats breakfast before heading out, leaving a

nearly full bowl of cereal in the sink and mumbling something about setting up job interviews and making contacts.

I linger over my cup of tea. At ten, I walk to Emmett's shop. It's time to end the nightly fantasies and see the man in person again. I have the built-in excuse of bringing his jacket back, and as I carry it folded over my arm, I resist the temptation to smell it. It's hard to believe it was cold enough for me to wear this a few weeks ago. It's hot and muggy now, more like summer than spring. The unseasonable heat is continuing, and the sun feels hard and heavy. I break out in an unfortunate sweat and sneak sniffs at my armpits, but I can't tell how well my deodorant is holding up.

I approach the shop with a surge of happiness and excitement. It's hardly a cute or inviting place. The walkway is swept clean, but the plain cement is cracked. The front door is solid black. The windows on either side are tinted and impossible to see through, and the neon sign above simply says TATTOOS.

I push open the door and the bell tinkles. The cool air feels wonderful on my damp skin.

Emmett glances over his shoulder at the sound. He nods as I come in, his usual laconic self, but I can tell he's glad to see me. I head to the back and place the jacket on an empty chair, then watch as he finishes up a dragonfly tattoo. It's small, with light and delicate lines. He's drawn it up high, near the girl's shoulder blade, and if I look quickly, it seems like a real insect is resting there for a moment.

"It looks really good," I tell her.

She smiles. She looks to be in her mid-twenties, with blond-streaked hair tousled around her pixieish face.

"Is this your first tattoo?" I ask.

"No, I have one on my hip."

"What is it?"

Emmett's finished, so after a quick glance at him to make sure it's okay to move, she shifts to her side and slides down her pants. There's a small four-leaf clover. To my untutored eye, it doesn't look as well inked as the dragonfly.

"It's for good luck," she says. "I'm Irish."

"How's that worked out for you?"

"Being Irish or my shamrock?"

"I don't know—both."

Emmett rolls his lips inward, as if trying to keep from smiling. In the meanwhile, he helps her to the long mirror so she can see the tattoo for herself. After her happy exclamations, he slathers her dragonfly in Vaseline, and then carefully tapes gauze over it. He gives her detailed instructions on how to care for the tattoo until the skin heals. She listens gravely and nods.

"I like my shamrock," she says, turning to me. "It keeps me grounded. But I needed another tattoo to remind me that sometimes I need to fly."

I really don't know what to say to this, so I smile and nod. I still don't understand how people believe that the drawing itself carries power. She pays for the tattoo, thanks Emmett again and leaves.

"You ask a lot of questions," he says.

"Oh, come on, that wasn't bad. I was just being friendly."

He wipes down the chair and starts cleaning his station, throwing away the used inks, putting the nondisposable equipment into the autoclave for sterilization.

"You throw all this stuff away? You barely used some of it."

"Great way to transmit disease," he says. "It's why some cities near naval bases banned tattoo parlors for a long time. Too many sailors catching too many things."

"That's gross."

"And the reason I'm throwing all these perfectly good inks away."

"So maybe it's not so wasteful."

He grunts slightly, acknowledging my concession.

"What brings you to my neck of the woods?" he says. "I haven't seen you in a while. Thought you moved on to another story."

"Missed me?"

"Yeah, I did," he says.

I pause for a second.

"I missed you too," I say softly, and take a deep breath. "It was kind of nice having your jacket; it reminded me of you."

He looks up from his cleaning, as though waiting for something.

But there's nothing else I'm ready to share. So after a moment, he nods and we share a smile.

"You are right, though," I say briskly, breaking up the suddenly intense atmosphere. "I have moved on to another story. It comes out next week; it's about this organic farm outside of town. It's also kind of my baby, since it's my own story idea."

"Congratulations," he says. Emmett has a way of lending

the simplest words a richness and depth they don't usually have. I squirm with pleasure at his simple felicitation.

"But don't worry," I say. "Just 'cause I have a new story doesn't mean we're not friends anymore." I need to get back to my more important project. "I still think you'd make a great personality profile, but Frank says we already have enough features for the next three months."

He gives me one of his searing, searching looks, then nods.

"So you're here for a tattoo?" he asks.

"No," I laugh. "Not yet." I deliberately look around the shop. We're the only ones in it. "Can I buy you a cup of coffee or something?"

He thinks about it for a moment, then shrugs. "It"s quiet today. And what's the point of owning my own business if I can't take off every once in a while?"

I grin widely and we set off into the heavy heat.

At the café, we settle at a small side table with our drinks, chatting about the Blank Pages—they have an album coming out. But then, as the small talk winds down, I take a deep breath and ease into the subject I've been waiting to touch on.

"I was wondering if you wanted to visit the office some-time," I say.

"At the newspaper?"

"Yeah. You know, I'm always hanging where you work; I thought you might want to see where I earn my honest wages."

He looks at me for a moment. "You are a strange one, Miriam."

"What?"

"You don't think that's kind of a weird thing to ask?"

"Well, first of all, no. I don't think so. I'm a naturally curious person; forgive me for assuming you were as well. But if you want to know the rest of the story, there's someone there I want you to meet."

"Trying to set me up?"

"No!" I'm ridiculously insulted and stung. Doesn't he remember that *I* like him?

He relaxes a fraction at my response.

"There's this kid, okay? An intern. I think he's got some issues—maybe his home life, maybe something at school. I don't know. I want to help him, but I can't get through to him. We started off on the wrong foot, and I think no matter what I do, I'm not 'cool enough,'" I say, making air quotes. "And . . . not to give you a big head, but you're the coolest person I know. In Hamilton."

He snorts at the qualification.

"I thought if I brought you in, maybe the three of us could hang out for a bit, get to know each other, and then maybe he'd loosen up around me."

"Why do you even care about this dude? He sounds like a loser."

I shrug. It's hard to put into words. "It's just this feeling that I'm supposed to help him. He acts like he's all bad, but I think there's something else going on underneath." At least there'd better be.

Emmett tips back his cup and finishes the last of his coffee.

"I need to get back to the shop." He puts down his mug

and rises. I stay in my seat, waiting for the rest of it. "Call me," he says. "I'll meet your boy."

"Sweet," I say, grinning up from my seat. "Thank you so much."

"Don't expect too much," he says darkly. "People have to want to be helped before you can help them."

He walks out and the door jangles loudly behind him.

The next day, I waste no time. As soon as I know for sure Jason's at the office, I call Emmett. He has a buddy visiting who can mind the shop while he takes off.

"I can give you an hour," he says. "But that's all."

We agree to meet at the coffee shop.

Getting Jason there is not easy.

He's hunched over the conference room table, his arm curved around a notebook as he furiously writes. His hair looks greasy, like he hasn't bathed in a while, but he doesn't smell bad. I wonder if he's using a weird kind of hair gel.

"Hey," I say casually. "I'm heading out to Higher Grounds for a break. You want to come?"

Warily, he looks up from his notebook.

"I'm Miriam," I remind him, but his closed expression doesn't change. "My treat," I offer.

Talking to him is like holding a tidbit of fish out to a feral cat, trying to lure him closer. As he shifts, I see a little of the notebook and realize he's been sketching, not writing. "You draw?" I ask, motioning toward the paper.

"No," he says flatly, closing the book.

I want to walk away so badly. He's rude; he's not interested.

It feels masochistic to keep pounding my head against the wall.

"Come on," I wheedle. "First of all, it's a free drink. Second, I've got someone I want you to meet. And third, besides the fact that it's totally rude to turn down a co-worker who asks you out for a coffee, it looks like there's nothing for you to do here today."

He sighs deeply. "Fine," he says.

"A man of few words. You're going to have to work on that if you want to be a reporter."

"I don't."

I stop for a second, but he brushes past me out the door. I follow, more perplexed than ever about what I'm supposed to do for him. And why him?

Jason perks up a bit at the sight of Emmett's tattoos and black motorcycle boots. But I don't know why I imagined the three of us chatting away and having a great ol' time. In fact, it's incredibly awkward as Emmett and I try to ask Jason about himself and he answers in monosyllables.

I'm about to write off this whole experiment as a total loss when I hear my name called. I turn and see Mo striding toward us.

"This is my brother." I introduce him all around, and without even waiting for an invitation, Mo pulls up an extra chair and joins us. He had seemed depressed when I went for work this morning, like a puppy getting left at home. He looks so happy to see me now that I don't have the heart to kick him under the table and tell him to leave.

He doesn't even bother ordering a drink at the counter.

At first I'm annoyed because, in typical Mo fashion, he completely takes over the conversation. Emmett glances at me once, then keeps his eyes on Mo and Jason. I wonder what he thinks of Mo. My brother is talking so fast that the words meld into each other as he tells all of us about his lousy interviews at a couple of attorney's offices he thought might be interested in a paid student intern position. Not surprisingly, they weren't receptive. I'm trying to think of ways to take back the conversation—questions to ask Jason to crack through that sullen grunt he prefers—when I finally realize that Mo's good-natured foul mouth is loosening up Jason. He smiles at Mo's self-deprecating humor and actually laughs when Mo turns his insults toward the firms he interviewed with. There's a gleam in Mo's eyes that tells me he's enjoying his own performance. He always appreciates a receptive audience. His laughter is sharp, almost a cackle. His words come fast, running into one another.

After a few minutes, Emmett rises. "I need to get back to the shop," he says. It hasn't been an hour yet. I tell Mo and Jason I'll be right back and hurry out after Emmett to thank him for coming.

"I don't think I was much help," he says.

I can see Mo and Jason through the window. Jason seems to be animated, talking about something that has Mo nodding in interest. This is the first time I've seen Jason speak to someone. I'm anxious to get back and hear what he's saying.

"You did better with him than I did. I can't believe that Mo's hitting it off so well with him."

"Your brother is . . ." He pauses, searching for the right word.

"I know," I say before he can find it. "We're twins."

Emmett shakes his head. "The mysteries of the world never cease."

"A lot of people say we look alike." I'm always defensive and protective of Mo. Besides, I don't want to have a long discussion right now about my brother's personality.

"There is a family resemblance. But it's not his looks I was thinking about. Though either one of you could hold a long, involved conversation with a brick wall."

"Hey!" I punch his arm; the muscles are flexed and hard.

He grins and dodges the next swing. Then he catches my hand and holds it gently. "But you're sweet," he says, and leaves the rest of his thought unspoken.

By the time I reenter the shop, Jason is pitching his drink into the trash can and the two of them are heading out.

"You guys leaving?" I say stupidly.

"Things to see, people to do," Mo says, kissing my cheek.

Jason doesn't bother answering.

I watch them leave the café, heads bent together like two old friends, talking excitedly about God knows what. Come to think of it, He probably does know what, but I have no idea. I have a feeling that when I question Mo tonight about it, he'll be vague and I'll be no closer to knowing what finally drew Jason out of his shell.

I try to ignore the very bad feeling in the pit of my stomach that this was not an accidental meeting. I keep waiting for

Mo to bring up the real reason he's here. But he's never hinted at anything about another mission. Maybe after successfully finishing his task, he's been left alone. Maybe. But that's only wishful thinking, and hope isn't much of a strategy.

Mo's sudden rapport with Jason feels bad. I just don't know who will suffer for it in the end: Jason, Mo or me.

XV.

TWO DAYS LATER, I'm prepping for my colonoscopy. I'm not supposed to eat anything and only drink clear liquids, and nothing red or purple. I stock up on Sprite, orange Gatorade, and chicken broth. That's the extent of the hardship until the afternoon, when I'm to drink the "tidal wave," a solution guaranteed to get my colon squeaky-clean.

I'm so humiliated by all this that I haven't told a soul—not Mo, not even my parents, definitely no one at work.

I head to the newsroom, sipping on a drink all morning. I heat a cup of broth for lunch and no one realizes I'm up to anything. I can't decide what I'm going to do in the evening once the waves start, since I don't want Mo to know. I told him that I have an assignment all day tomorrow and not to expect me.

The doctor did say I wouldn't be able to drive myself

home after the procedure, but I figure I'll call a cab, come home and crash.

Self-pity is too close to the surface, and the less I think about it, the less I have to deal with my new reality. And there's this abiding sense of shame. A feeling that I'm being punished for being bad. Maybe once I have a diagnosis, I'll talk. Then again, maybe I won't.

Fortunately, I don't have to make up a reason for Mo to leave the apartment. He isn't there when I come home from work, and as the solution kicks in and I'm racing to the toilet every twenty minutes, I don't have time or energy to wonder where he is or what he's up to.

After what feels like days, weeks—after everything I ever ate or ever will eat is cleared out—I realize two things. One: this would make a very effective method of torture. Two: any celebrity who voluntarily undergoes a colonic should be committed to a mental institution.

The next morning I drive to the clinic. There's a large waiting room, but I'm quickly called to the back by a nurse, who leads me to a changing room. I strip, placing all my clothes in a large plastic bag, put on a drafty gown and pad out in my socks. The nurse, a tired-looking middle-aged woman, takes my worldly possessions and stuffs them on a rack under the hospital gurney. I clamber onto it, holding closed my flapping gown, trying not to flash anyone. The nurse waits until I settle in place and then puts in an IV. It's cold in the room, and I hug myself with one arm as I shiver, keeping the IV arm straight.

"Poor little thing," the nurse says when she notices. "I'll

see if I can find you a blanket or something. They do keep it mighty cold in here."

The IV is hooked up to a saline bag that drips cold, clear drops at a regular interval, chilling my whole arm. My stomach is completely empty: no solid food since the day before yesterday, nothing to drink since last night. My teeth are nearly chattering. But really, it isn't the cold.

I'm shaking with fear.

After a twenty-minute wait, I'm wheeled to a small room jammed with various machines. I'm pale, and on the monitor counting my heartbeats, I see my heart is shuddering at ninety-five beats a minute.

Dr. Messa walks in, with two assistants close behind him. The tiny room, no bigger than a walk-in closet, is now packed. If I wasn't on the gurney, I wouldn't fit.

"Well, Miss Abbot-Levy, let's see what we've got here, shall we?"

I manage to pull my lips up in a ghastly semblance of a smile.

"Lay on your left side, sweetheart," the nurse says. "Now pull your knees toward your chest."

I follow orders, gritting my teeth. I breathe through my nose, fighting to stay calm. My heart rate is now over a hundred beats a minute. Curling on my left side makes the gown fall open in the back. I fight the urge to grab for it. I fight the urge to hop off the gurney and make a break for the door. I'm completely exposed, and the position causes what my yoga teacher would call "the blossoming of the seat."

I see Dr. Messa take a syringe and plunge its contents into

the IV line. I feel a hand on my back as the nurse pats me reassuringly and places an instrument on the bed behind me and then . . . a rush of static in my brain . . . and nothing else registers.

An indeterminate amount of time later, I wake up in a tiny, curtained-off cell. I hear people murmuring near me, so there must be others waking up from procedures all around me. I feel very relaxed and a bit light-headed, but in a good way. I'm not hungry, just very mellow.

After I pass a few minutes placidly staring at the stripes on the curtains, a nurse peeks in. It's not the same one from before.

"You're awake," she says. "How do you feel?"

"Sleepy."

"That's normal," she says briskly. "The doctor will be here soon. Who's coming to pick you up?"

"Just take a cab," I murmur.

"Oh no," she says loudly, riled up. "You can't do that. Didn't you read your packet?"

Some of the mellowness is fading in the face of her ire, but I'm determined to hold on to it. This is the best I've felt in weeks.

"It said I'm not supposed to drive," I say calmly. I'm not going to let this skinny, frizzy-haired woman take away this blissful peace any sooner than it has to go.

"No ma'am," she says. "We cannot release you to a taxi. It's against the law. You have to have someone you know and trust drive you home. You could get robbed, or God knows what." Even in my mushy state, I know that what she says isn't enforceable. They can't keep me here against my will. And what if the taxicab driver was my friend? But it's too hard to muster up a fight.

"Don't you know anyone who'll come get you?" Her tone implies that I must be even more pathetic than she first thought. As much as I hate condescending endearments, I suddenly realize they are not the worst thing after all. I could use a "sweetheart" or "honey" right now. I want my mom.

Mo doesn't have a car.

"Call Emmett," I say. "The tattoo shop on East Cannon."

She humpfs at me and leaves, twitching the curtain closed behind her.

I shut my eyes and try to drift back to that sweet, mellow state, but it's already fading.

When I hear the curtains sliding, I assume it's the nurse again, but when I open my eyes, Dr. Messa is rolling a stool over to sit next to me. He's holding a folder and he looks serious.

"Miriam, how are you feeling?"

"I'm fine," I lie. My heart rate has picked up again. This won't be good news.

"The findings from the scope, the evidence of ulcers and inflammation, along with your symptoms, mean that I am now confident in my diagnosis. I've taken biopsies, which I've sent to a lab, and those will take a few days to come back. But it's safe to say you have Crohn's disease."

He places the folder on his lap and opens it. There are

bright color photos of what, even to my untrained eye, are obviously pictures of the inside of my colon. I feel myself blush. I want to cover them, for decency's sake.

Dr. Messa doesn't notice my distress. He discusses various parts of the photos, explaining what a normal lining looks like, showing what mine looks like. Pointing out the individual ulcers—the cause, apparently, of all my misery. They don't look awful. They don't look like they should cause sleepless nights of agony.

He's talking, but at some point I don't hear the words anymore.

Eventually, with no questions from me, Dr. Messa closes the folder and rises.

"You might not remember everything about this conversation," he says. "If you have any questions, call the office. In fact, go ahead and call tomorrow and make an appointment. I'm writing a prescription right now for Asacol, which you'll need to take in the morning and at night. It might be that's all we need to keep your symptoms in check. If you don't see an improvement in two weeks, we'll discuss further options.

"I've included some packets for you to read about your disease. They should help you understand what's going on, and the implications of this diagnosis." He pauses, looking expectantly at me. I nod, though I'm not sure what he wants from me.

"I'm told your ride will be here soon. You're free to go as soon as he arrives."

He pats my hand, the first humane gesture he's shown me, and then walks out, leaving the curtain open.

The same frizzy-haired nurse comes in. She takes out the IV and wordlessly bends down, reaching under the gurney and yanking out the bag with my clothes. She hands me the bag, and after making sure I can stand on my own two feet without collapsing, she leaves, pulling the curtain behind her.

I dress slowly. Every movement careful, like a drunk or someone afraid of falling. Putting my own clothes back on helps ease the sense of disassociation, but still, I'm lost.

I have Crohn's. I am a crone. I'm sick. I am diseased. Medicine. Implications. Every word feels heavy and nauseating.

I want my mellow numbness back. I want to sleep forever.

"Miriam, can I come in?"

Emmett's deep voice is incongruent here.

"Sure," I say. But my voice cracks and I have to say it again. "Come in."

He pushes the curtain aside, filling up the space with health and strength.

"What a fun morning you've been having," he says. "I can't believe you almost didn't invite me."

It's the perfect thing to say. I smile.

"Are you ready to split?" he asks.

I nod.

"Then let's go."

I walk very slowly, but he seems in no hurry. For some reason, I can't make my legs move quickly. After a moment, without asking, he takes my hand and I grip his tightly. I don't look around. I don't care where I'm going. I just follow him down some corridors, past various doors and finally outside to the parking lot.

He opens the car door for me, closes it once I'm inside, then gets in and drives without asking questions. I close my eyes and doze.

When the car comes to a stop, I realize we're at the back of his shop, at the entrance to his apartment.

He catches my look.

"They said you shouldn't be left alone today. Easier to keep an eye on you if you're here. If that's okay?"

"Okay," I say.

Some of the mellowness has returned. I want the name of whatever Dr. Messa put in my IV. It's wonderful.

I climb up the stairs, with Emmett right behind me. Without waiting for an invitation, I kick off my shoes and crawl into his bed. The sheets are cool and they smell like him.

I dive into sleep like an alcoholic stepping into a pub. This is where I need to be.

I sleep for maybe an hour. When I wake, my neck hairs are standing on end and I know immediately I'm not alone. But Emmett's not here. His steady, caring gaze is gone. Someone, or rather something, else is here.

Miriam! a voice booms in my head. *Miriam! Arise and look before thee!*

I sit bolt upright, clutching the sheets as Emmett's room disappears. My ears are ringing from the command and my eyes widen as I realize I'm looking at a courtroom with a trial in session. I catch a fleeting glimpse of Jason in the defendant's chair, his face stony, his whole attitude cold and sneering as he leans back. He is wearing a brand-new coat and tie. Then I see Judge Bender presiding from his seat on high. The courtroom is packed with spectators, and it takes me a moment before I realize the judge is sentencing Jason.

I'm woozy with motion sickness, or something like it. I cannot tell where my body begins; it's almost as if I've lost it during the transfer here. The vision, if that's what this is, isn't clear. It's like looking at something underwater. Sizes shift, magnified and minimized, blurry and clear, like someone's adjusting the focus. I see the avid, hungry looks of the spectators, like a mob at a witch trial. Then I hear the judge. I focus on him; his face is florid against his long black robes. His eyes gleam with righteous satisfaction. The picture warps less now that I'm looking at him. My view of the judge makes me think that I am sitting in the jury box. But there is no jury, just me.

"I hereby sentence you to five consecutive life terms," he announces. I hear a muffled response from the spectators, but I don't turn to look. He bangs his gavel five times, the booms echoing oddly in my ears. "Jason Way, for the crime you have committed, for the blight that your presence is on society, for the threat you will always pose wherever you are, you will be locked away in a cell for the rest of your natural life."

I turn to look at Jason. His expression hasn't changed, and I realize this is the outcome he expected. What heinous crime has he committed? In what is part lecture, part sermon, Judge Bender continues.

"Deviants like you force the rest of us to put up walls. You force us to take steps to enforce the most basic, fundamental laws common to all God-fearing societies. The repercussions of your actions will reverberate through our town, our state and our country." My brain is racing, trying to figure out what this means. Is this a vision of the future? Is this what I'm supposed to save Jason from? "One day, after many, many years of contemplation," the judge thunders, "you will face a judgment greater than mine. And when you do, may God show greater mercy on you. . . ." My mind is struggling to think. What did he do? When will this terrible crime happen?

As if the power that brought me this vision can tell I'm no longer paying attention, or perhaps because I've seen all I need to see, as suddenly as it all began, it's over. I'm back in Emmett's bed, the sheets tangled around me like ropes, my heart pounding like I've run a race.

I flop back on the bed, gasping for breath. I frantically try to think. Jason's only a teenager, a surly, maladjusted boy, true, but not a vicious one. What horrible crime could he possibly commit in the near future? What can I do to stop him?

But the drug is still in my system and it pulls me under. I fight it, but my thoughts grow more and more sluggish. Against my will, my body relaxes. My eyelids droop. And my racing thoughts fade to nothing.

XVI.

When I wake again, the afternoon sun is streaming through a gap in the curtains. I lie still for a moment, blinking at the ceiling, assessing how I feel. I slowly sit up and look around the room. As always, there's nothing to show that my vision wasn't some painkiller-induced nightmare. Except that I do know better now. I feel sick to my stomach. Someone has given me a swift kick in the pants. Clearly, I'm not doing enough and that needs to change.

I chew on a fingernail, wondering what to do. What with my new diagnosis, the vision, my lack of success in getting to know Jason and Mo butting in, I'm at a loss for what to worry about first. When my stomach grumbles, a more immediate concern becomes clear. I'm starving.

It's been thirty-six hours since I've had a solid meal, and I've had nothing to drink all day. So I'm not only hungry, I'm parched as well. As I swing my legs over the side of the bed, I notice a glass of water on the nightstand. I gulp it down, the cool water sliding down my throat.

Wearing the same loose drawstring pants and soft cotton shirt that I wore to the procedure, I pad downstairs in bare feet, holding the empty glass. I find Emmett in the small kitchen tucked behind the shop. We're both surprised to see each other, but he recovers first, coming to take the glass from me and carefully looking at my face.

"I'm okay," I say.

"You slept for so long I called the doctor. He said if you didn't wake up by three to call back. It's five minutes till."

At the mention of the doctor, I frown a bit. I'm not ready to deal with that yet. I wish the morning's news were a bad dream I could brush away. But then again, my bad dreams can't be brushed away either, so it's really hopeless.

"I'm starving. Are you cooking something?"

He accepts the change of subject. "I figured you'd want something easy on the belly. Do scrambled eggs and toast sound all right?"

"Mmm, tasty." My mouth waters at the thought of food. "Can I help?"

"Sit and watch," he says, heading to the fridge and pulling out four eggs.

"I can do that."

I sit at one of the two stools beside a tiny round table and watch him. Like with everything else I've seen him do, he's wonderfully competent in the kitchen. In clean, quick movements he cracks the eggs with one hand, whisking them with the other. With his back turned to me and his attention focused on the eggs, I take this moment to get another good look at his tattoos. I can't seem to get enough of them. I could ask about them, but I don't. If I ask questions, then he might too.

He plates the steaming eggs next to golden toast and places the dish in front of me. He then sits down with his own plate. I like that he made some for himself too. I hate eating when other people aren't.

I ask about the shop. We make small talk. We eat our food.

"Saw your buddy Jason yesterday," he says. "Hanging out with Mo."

At Jason's name, the eggs curdle in my mouth. It takes an effort, but I swallow them.

"Really?" I say casually.

Had Mo spent all of yesterday with him? I'd been so relieved that Mo wasn't in the apartment that I never thought what he was up to. A part of me thinks that I should give Mo the benefit of the doubt. If Mo gets Jason to open up, then I've a better chance to break through as well. And unlike me, Mo might not have any ulterior motives in getting to know Jason better. But I can't deny that I'm uncomfortable with this new friendship. I am worried for Mo, but also scared of what he could do. It's hard to think of him as an adversary, yet until I know where Mo stands with the devil, I can't trust him. And now that I know Jason's on the brink of a horrible crime, Mo's interest in Jason is even more disturbing. I push away my plate. I've only eaten half my portion, but my stomach is uncomfortably full and I've lost my appetite.

"I've been asking around a bit," Emmett continues. "Your buddy Jason is an interesting character. He goes to Warfield, did you know that?"

I nod. All the paper's interns come from Warfield. Hamilton has a very well-respected public school system, something the town is quite proud of. But despite this, Warfield is where anyone with any aspirations to the town's upper class sends their kids.

"I thought that was strange. Jason's not exactly a Warfield poster child," Emmett continues. Which is so true, and something that I hadn't really thought about. Warfield students are all rich preppies, usually driving brand-new Mustang convertibles or giant Dodge Rams. Not to generalize, but they all seem to have that subtle superior smirk that suggests they are secretly laughing at you. Jason, with his hip-hop clothes, snarky manners and awful hair, is as out of place with the Lacoste crowd as a plastic spork at Williams-Sonoma.

"Maybe he's there on scholarship," I say, getting interested despite my grim mood.

"But the scholarship kids at Warfield are unreal," he says. "They're either athletes, world-class athletes—Warfield has sent two kids to the Olympic trials—or they're brainiacs, scary-brilliant kids. Doing college physics in the tenth grade. One girl published a novel. They're so smart it's ridiculous. And then we have Jason. . . ."

He lets that hang in the air.

"He might be really smart," I say. "He got the newspaper internship."

Emmett gives me a look.

"Some geniuses have very poor social skills. It's the whole social IQ thing, totally separate from intellectual IQ."

Again Emmett gives me a look.

"Okay, fine," I say. "He's a jerk. He's not athletic, he's not scary smart. He doesn't come from a rich family. What's he doing at Warfield?"

"Exactly," Emmett says, with a smug smile that says I'm finally catching on. "So it turns out, he's not there on scholarship. They don't waste them on losers. His mom pays full tuition. And she's a mail carrier."

"Wait, how much is tuition?" I'd assumed it was crazy high, but maybe I was wrong.

"Fifteen grand a year." Okay, so I wasn't wrong. My university didn't cost that much.

"Ouch." I think for a minute. "And how much does a mail carrier make?"

Emmett makes a face. "Forty? Fifty a year?"

I think about what it would mean to have your mom spend more than a fifth of her income on your high school tuition.

"I bet she has high hopes for her son," I say. I don't know if it's some lingering effect of the drug or knowing what's in store for Jason, but I'm suddenly crystal-clear on Jason's situation. "I bet she's always telling him that he's going places, don't you think? Can't you just hear her say that he's going to be someone really important one day?"

"And I bet his schoolmates prove to him every day that she's wrong," rumbled Emmett. I think about my vision and Jason's future. I don't like where this is heading.

I glance at Emmett, wondering for the first time what sort of person he was in high school, which group he belonged to: goth, jock, druggie, nerd, prep—he doesn't fit in any easy category. It's hard to imagine him being bullied, but there's a bitter, knowing tinge to his voice that suggests otherwise.

"So let's assume he's an outcast," I say, following this train of thought. "A total loser, letting his mom down. Maybe he hates her for putting him where he doesn't belong, for expecting all these things of him that she never expected from herself. . . ." I'm thinking out loud, hardly censoring my words. "Does he hate her or does he just hate himself? How am I supposed to help him? What am I supposed to do for him?"

"Why do you have to do anything?" Emmett asks.

My obsession with Jason perplexes him. I shouldn't have said so much, and I can't think of a good explanation. Looking down at my hands, I see the outline of the tape that held the IV from this morning. I rub it self-consciously.

"This morning, I was diagnosed with Crohn's," I say. He thinks I'm changing the subject, but really I'm not. "The doctor kind of thought that's what's wrong with me, so I've been reading about it before this procedure. It's an autoimmune disease. It means my body's immune system has gone nuts and is now attacking me. In my case, it's attacking my colon, shredding it, destroying it. But it could attack any part of my digestive system. If we can't find the right medicine to stop it, my own immune system will kill me. There is no cure," I huff with silent, bitter laughter.

Emmett stays perfectly still, listening intently, like he's scared to spook me.

"So I've been thinking a lot about our bodies, how complicated they are, how there's so much we don't know about how things work, why things work the way they do. And I've been thinking about God. We don't really think about how much we owe to God—I mean, our existence, our lives, our bodies. People used to think that when things went wrong, when disease came, it was God's will, His punishment. And now we say it's a virus or it's genetics or it's pollution. But maybe it's all the same thing, you know?"

He doesn't nod or shake his head.

"It sounds crazy. I think you have to be sick, you have to be scared, before you can move past this religion of science we all grew up with. But why is it that even when there are known carcinogens in a certain area, not everyone gets sick? When there was the plague and medicine was as primitive as could be, not everyone got sick, and of the sick, not everyone died." He doesn't answer, and I talk faster so he can't interrupt. "Maybe God *does* have something to do with that. And if that's the case and you're sick, maybe you have an obligation to try and figure how to right any wrongs you might have done. How to uncross God, how to appease Him. How to be worthy of His gifts."

I risk a glace up at him and he looks so sad. I ball up my napkin, twisting it in my lap. Slowly he reaches out and covers my tightly clenched hands with his. His hands are warm and heavy, and they still my nervous wringing. I swallow a lump in my throat.

"I don't believe God works that way," he says softly. "I don't think He uses our bodies to punish us, to whip us in line like mules."

I start to say something, but he continues.

"If I had to guess, I'd say we disappoint Him very often. Though after so many centuries, maybe He's lowered His standards a bit." He shrugs. "Maybe not. I don't know. But if you believe in free will, which I do, then God has to let us stumble along blindly, making our choices, reaping their fruit. If there is some kind of a reckoning—punishment for bad choices, reward for good ones—it's in the afterlife, not here.

"I'm sorry that you're sick. I'm very, very sorry," he says, touching my hair softly. "But when we get sick, that's just living in this imperfect world. That's molecules and DNA and bacteria doing what they've been programmed to do, and it's up to us to bear it and fight it and hopefully triumph over it.

"I don't think you're going to be able to buy God's indulgence, to earn a pardon or early release for good behavior."

I rise from my seat and his hands fall away. I swipe at the tears spilling down my face.

"You're wrong," I say, my voice nearly strangled with tears. "I did something wrong and then I got sick. If I do something right, this will go away." My chin is quivering like mad. If I open my lips again, the only thing that will come out will be bawling howls of miserable fear. So I button them tight and don't look at the pity I know is on his hard face.

He accepts the end of the discussion, and silently we clear the dishes. As I gather my things for him to drive me home, he says one last thing:

"Everyone has burdens and everyone has made mistakes, Miriam."

"Yes," I say. "I know."

I can't afford to make another one.

XVII.

EMMETT DROPS ME OFF at my empty apartment. Mo's out again.

While I'm not telling my parents about the colonoscopy and diagnosis, I feel an urgent need to hear their voices.

I call my mom first. But after the preliminary "I'm fine, and how are you?" I find myself hoping for better answers.

"I think I'm having a crisis of faith," I say.

"Are you doubting God's existence again?" my mother asks. In the family lore, I break out crying at age seven at the dinner table. "It's the monkeys! How can there be God if we come from monkeys? Which is it? Adam or Koko?"

"No." I laugh hollowly. "I don't doubt His existence. I am inundated with signs and wonders. I just don't *like* Him very much."

"Ah well, now, that's a different problem altogether, isn't

it?" my mother says comfortably, not at all perturbed. "You are in good company. There isn't a man or woman of faith who hasn't had a complaint or two about God. Life has a way of throwing us uncatchable lobs of misery. We tend to blame God for it, but usually in hindsight you can see things differently." I hear the sounds of dishes clanking in the background. She must be tidying up after her tea.

"Mom, I'm not talking about a bad grade or a car accident. It's bigger, deeper, than that, and I do hold God directly responsible."

"Darling." The multitasking clanking stops for a moment. "Has something happened? What's wrong?"

I stop to take a deep breath. I feel such a need to unburden myself, but I cannot find the words.

"I'm just frustrated with where my life is going," I say lamely. "I try to do the right thing, but half the time I don't even know what that is. And it's not like anyone thanks me for it, anyway."

I hear a soft chuckle. I do sound so young and silly complaining like that.

"My dear, welcome to adulthood in shades of gray."

"Lovely," I say, dripping with sarcasm.

She laughs. And in her kind, patient voice, she continues: "You know that I have always believed we are God's vessels. Perhaps you don't like what's before you, but that only means you've lost your perspective. Something to think about, no?"

I sigh. "It is. Well, don't let anyone say you give out easy answers."

She laughs again. "I have never been accused of that

before. You know, this reminds me of a wonderful verse: 'This is love for God: to obey his commands. And his commands are not burdensome.' I John 5:3."

I listen to her voice on the line, the stunningly simple words that encapsulate everything.

"I often turn to that when I feel a bit overcome. We aren't given anything we can't bear. And once you realize that, nothing seems as bad as it used to."

"Do you really believe that?" I rub a hand across my stomach.

"I do. I really do. I love you, sweetheart."

"I love you too, Mom."

The next morning, I'm back at work. It's my second day on the medicine and there's no change in my symptoms so far. I push aside lingering worries of divine compensations and consequences, because regardless of all that, I have a mission.

There's clearly more to Jason's story than what Emmett discovered, and I'm not a journalist for nothing. I've got sources. When Frank, wearing a pale linen suit, bustles into his office, I rise and follow him.

I knock on the door and poke my head in.

"You got a minute?"

Frank looks up from the cup of coffee in his hand and at the papers strewn on his desk. "Sure, Miriam, come on in."

I move some folders off the visitor's chair in Frank's remarkably cluttered office and take a seat.

"The Sweetwater piece runs tomorrow," he says. "You did a nice job."

"Great." A twinge of excitement zings through me.

He shuffles some papers and then hands one to me. "Our next get-to-know-you is on Judge Bender."

My breath catches for a moment at the judge's name. I make a face. "I feel like I need a chaperone to be in the same room as him."

"He's a pussycat," Frank says, waving an arm languidly. "Just a good ol' southern boy."

I make a noncommittal sound. The image of Judge Bender sentencing Jason with unabashed relish flashes through my mind.

"He's going to be a national player one of these days," Frank adds pragmatically. "He won't do anything to jeopardize that."

That's a kind of comfort, I suppose, but before I can think of some sort of sarcastic reply to that bit of news, Frank tells me he received two e-mails about my piece on the farmers' market and he's planning to publish one of them as a letter to the editor. As he's full of praise for me, and hopefully in a chatty mood, I leap into the real reason I came.

"Listen, I want to talk to you about something," I say.

Catching something serious in my tone of voice, chatty Frank suddenly seems antsy, and sure enough, I catch him sneaking a look at his watch and then turning to me.

"I do have several appointments today. . . ." He leaves the dismissal unspoken.

"It won't take long," I promise, and waste no more time. "I just need to know, what's the story with Jason?"

"Oh, not you too," he says testily, his usual genial manner evaporating. "I have my reasons for hiring Jason, and he's only here for a couple of months, so just deal with it, okay?"

This outburst is so unlike the amiable Frank that I stare at him in surprise.

"I do like him," I say.

"You do?"

I laugh at the shock in his voice.

"Well, I think I could like him if I got to know him better," I hedge. "I took him out for a cup of coffee a couple of days ago, but . . . uh . . . let's just say he keeps his cards close to his chest." That's the nicest way I can think of to describe Jason's unique combination of surly yet silent blankness, and I'm rather pleased with myself for coming up with it.

Frank thinks for a moment, then nods. "All right, you bloodhound. Close the door and I'll tell you his story."

I hop out of my seat and do as he says, then lean close, expecting some juicy gossip. Instead, I hear a variation on the themes I've already heard from Emmett. Jason is struggling in school; he doesn't fit in. Doesn't have many friends. Jason's mother, according to Frank, expects to be raising a future senator from Tennessee. I vigorously suppress any eye-rolling, snorts or raised eyebrows of disbelief.

"That must be hard," I say.

"It is; it's very hard on a young boy," Frank says, a little too piously. "Dave Finely, the principal at Warfield, came to me asking that Jason have this internship as a personal favor to him." He emphasizes "personal."

"What do you get out of it?"

186

He grins a Cheshire cat grin, smug and mysterious, but doesn't answer at first. At least he's not offended by the question.

"It's a civic duty," he finally says, self-righteously. "The boy is interested in illustration and is an avid reader, though between you and me, the only thing I ever see the child read is pulp fiction or comic books." He grimaces. "We thought landing the internship, exposure to a career that he shows some natural inclination toward—I wouldn't say aptitude—might help him find his place in this world."

"But . . ." But I already know the answer. Jason is not thriving at the paper any more than he is at school.

"But the boy has a remarkable ability to aggravate every soul he comes in contact with," Frank finishes grimly. Whatever the Warfield principal promised, I have a feeling Frank will demand extra for pain and suffering. "You're the first person who hasn't marched in here demanding I let him go. In fact," he says, with a sudden gleam in his eye, "since you like him so much, I'll make him your assistant. Yes, that's it." The solution found, the lines around Frank's eyes and mouth lighten.

Frank misreads the stunned expression on my face.

"He just doesn't know how to express affection, is all," Frank says, not even caring how ridiculous that sounds. He's too happy to have solved his office problem. "He's yours now, Miriam; teach him well. Take him along on assignments; have him write your headlines; show him the ropes." The phone rings, and Frank looks delighted at the fortuitous end to our meeting. "Nice chatting with you," he says as he reaches to answer the phone. "Stop by anytime. . . . Frank Hale here," he says, picking up the receiver. "Betty, wonderful to hear from you." He makes a shooing motion with his hand and swivels his chair so his back is to me. "About the fund-raiser you wanted us to cover . . ."

I leave his office in a state of euphoria, amazed at my luck and thrilled about this turn of events. Jason will have to hang around me while at the paper, and the more time I have to chip away at the brick wall he's built around himself, the more likely the chance I will break through.

At my desk, I make a list of things we could do together, activities that might inspire him and, if nothing else, force him to spend time with me and let me get to know him better. But reading over my list—*What's your idea of the perfect news-paper article? Name five issues this paper should cover*—I grow depressed. The list sounds like a cross between a really bad summer camp and a school assignment. I try to think of some-thing better, something cooler, but don't come up with much. At any rate, Jason is a no-show that afternoon, so I have time to devise a better strategy.

When I arrive home, I'm surprised to find Mo. I haven't seen him in days, and he looks a bit grungy and tired.

"Hey, sis," he says, closing the fridge and turning toward me. "Long time, stranger."

"I know; I was ready to call the police. Or Mom and Dad." He shudders.

"Where have you been?" I ask.

"Oh, you know." He lopes over to the couch and flops down. "Just hanging out. Chillin'."

I set down on the kitchen table the messenger bag I use as

my briefcase and notice the crumbs and smears he's left. There are dirty dishes in the sink. I feel like a bad parody of a 1950s housewife. I don't say anything about the messy kitchen.

"You got plans for tonight?" I ask. With him gone so much of the time, I've been lonely for his company. I want to know what he's up to, but I also want to hang out with my brother, who, for all his flaws, can make anything fun.

"Sorry, sis," he says, with a quick grin to show he knows he's disappointing me. "Already booked."

"Can I come?"

He blinks in surprise. "Sure, it's a Mortal Kombat tournament. You up for that?"

Mo was never much for video games, and I wonder about this odd new hobby.

"Are you lying to me?" I ask softly.

He's shocked for a second before he recovers.

"That was rude," he says, giving me a look. "This group of guys I met, we hang out and play, like, all night long. It's crazy."

"It's fun?" This is so strange, so unlike Mo—who's always moving and plotting and active—that I can't even wrap my mind around it. I hate myself for my growing suspicion, for the mistrust that must be showing on my face.

For a second there, Mo's smirky mask falls and he looks tired, the way you'd look after you'd studied all night but were still unprepared for the final exam. Then he visibly pulls himself back together and shrugs, shutting me out. "It's a guy thing," he says dismissively. "Don't wait up."

On his way out, he gives me a big hug. I hug him back,

but not as tightly. I'm so confused. I almost believe him. He pulls away and, without a backward glance, heads out.

The apartment feels echoey and empty. I really don't want an evening of eating a microwave dinner, watching a show and going to bed.

On impulse, I call Trudy.

"Hi, beautiful," she says, her cheerful voice already making me feel better. "I hope you're not calling to say the article was canceled, because I've been telling everyone we're going to be famous."

"Just the opposite," I assure her. "I found out today that the piece will be published tomorrow. I didn't want you to miss it."

We chat for a bit—I tell her about the nice letters to the editor about the farmers' market story—and maybe she's feeling generous, maybe she can hear I sound lonely, but just when I think our conversation is about to end, she invites me over for dinner.

"What, tonight?"

"Sure," she laughs. "We're harvesting, and then having a big cookout for the interns. You don't look like you eat more than a mouthful, and we're cooking like an army's coming. Join us. Our intern Rebecca is in town picking up supplies; she can pick you up on her way back."

"Okay," I say, delighted. "That sounds like a lot of fun. Can I bring anything?"

"Just your pretty face. We have more food here than we know what to do with."

Following the same impulse that had me calling Trudy in

the first place, I ask, "In that case, is it okay if I invite a friend to come along?"

"The more the merrier," she says in her glad voice. "See you soon."

I call Emmett.

"I have a proposition," I say.

"You sound better than yesterday." His voice is rich and deep, rumbling in my ear and shimmying straight down my chest. Again I am struck with a surprised sort of joy that he cares about me, that he notices.

"That's because I've had a much better day," I say. I think about the progress made at the paper, about going out to the farm. I don't think about Mo and his mysterious rendezvous. "You know that organic farm I was telling you about?" He makes an affirmative sound. "Do you want to help harvest veggies and have dinner there?"

He thinks for a moment. I can hear papers being shuffled.

"Do you have to work at the shop?" I ask, already disappointed. I feel consumed by the sudden desire that he come. In my head I'm chanting, *Say yes, say yes, say yes.* "It'll be so nice, and you'll love Trudy and Hank."

"Sure," he says. "Sounds good."

"Great! Rebecca and I will come by and pick you up," I say before he can change his mind. "See you in a bit."

Rebecca, a lavender-scented intern with closely trimmed hair, drives a rickety farm truck that's loaded with empty harvest boxes. Emmett and I end up clearing a small space next to the cab in the open bed. We hunker down, braced against opposite corners, and hold on to the hard metal sides for the duration of the ride.

It's oddly thrilling to ride in the open bed. No roof, no windows, no seat belts. Rebecca is a careful driver, especially with us in the back, but the turns still sway me from side to side and the odd bumps and potholes sometimes knock my head back against the cab's glass window, causing Rebecca to shout, "Sorry! Are you okay?"

Wearing dark cargo pants, boots and a tight shirt, Emmett looks remarkably at ease in this unorthodox ride, and he seems to weather the turns and bumps better. But like me, he does knock his head a couple of times. His expressions of surprise and disgruntlement cause me to break out in a bad case of the giggles.

I'm wearing old jeans with holes at the knees, battered tennis shoes and a faded blue tank top. I'm not trying to be sexy, or cool, or anything else I'm probably not anyway. I'm relaxed and comfortable, and I love that he's here with me. It's too windy and loud to talk, so I alternate between enjoying the lovely rolling green hills, the farms and pastured horses that we pass, and sneaking glances at Emmett because as lovely as the countryside is, he's even more appealing.

After we bump along the farm's dirt driveway, keeping our heads well away from the metal sides and the window, and help unload the empty boxes, we're quickly directed to a field with an extralarge collard green harvest. We get a crash course in proper harvesting technique as Trudy squats and snaps the large green leaves close to the main stalk. Leaves will regrow off that main stalk and yield more harvests. After watching us snap the first few, Trudy hurries off to attend to the other chores on her list. Everyone spreads out, staking out a row. It's fun at first as I fill my basket, but after a while it stops being fun and starts being work. The sun is so low that it seems to shine straight into my eyes, giving me a headache. The mosquitoes come out as dusk falls, and I stop more and more often to slap at whining sounds and bites.

Trudy comes by to check on my progress and hums approvingly at my three-quarters-full basket.

"We'll make a farmer out of you yet," she says. She hands me a water bottle and I gratefully drink from it.

"Harder than it looks," I say sheepishly after I come up for air.

"Now, isn't that the truth." Trudy digs her fists against her lower back and moans. "Farming is for the young," she says. "Too bad y'all are too young to see that. No offense."

My hands are caked in dirt, my hair is hanging in sweaty, lanky clumps around my sunburned face and my young back is throbbing from crouching down at collard level.

"None taken," I say. I'm rather in awe that she subjects herself to this day after day, year after year.

Trudy wanders off to check on the other pickers, and I look around for Emmett. I find him hard at work two rows away. In quick, efficient movements he snaps the wide green leaves and stacks them in his basket. After we finish harvesting, we'll take our baskets back to the house and bundle the leaves in bunches with rubber bands. I can't resist spending time with Emmett, so I heft my basket and make my way over. As soon as I draw near, he straightens from his crouch and wipes a heavy, colorful arm across his forehead.

"Wicked hard work," he says. Sweat is running down the side of his face, and his shirt is drenched with dark stains under his arms, down his chest and across his back.

"Are you getting sunburned?"

"Nah, just dehydrated."

"Here, finish it." I hand him the half-empty water bottle and he drains it.

"My grandparents used to have a huge garden," he says. "My sister and I hated it. It seemed like there was always something that needed to be done there." We both survey the field.

"It's more work than I ever thought," I admit. "You don't think when you go to the grocery store for veggies that people put in so much time and labor to get them there for you."

"Yeah, it's true," he says. "And I hated all the work when I was a kid. But man, tomato soup from roasted garden tomatoes? There is nothing better on earth." There's no place to toss trash, so he tucks the empty bottle into a deep side pocket of his cargo pants.

"My mom has a beautiful garden at her house, but it's mostly flowers," I say. "She grows herbs, but that's about it for edible plants. And she does it mainly for their scent."

"My grandparents were way too practical for flowers," Emmett says. I can hear the fondness and exasperation in his voice. "My grandmother would sneak in a hibiscus or gardenia every once in a while, but most of the garden was for sustenance. Cabbage, potatoes, pole beans, tomatoes, cucumbers, squash. You name it, we grew it. Except for in the hottest part of summer, we'd have vegetables from our garden, and in the summer, we'd eat what Gran had canned. I grew up in Florida," he adds. "So our growing season was ass-backwards. Winter was the fertile time; summer was fallow."

I'm eating up his words, picturing how different his childhood was from mine.

"But even in the summer, we'd have mangoes, lychees and watermelons; they don't mind the heat. Which sounds great, until you realize that picking fruit in the summer means mosquitoes swarming over you and crows fighting for the fruit." He wipes his face again, using the bottom of his shirt. I try not to ogle his abs. "It's easy to look back and see it as idyllic, but I remember how much my sister and I fought over garden chores."

"You probably would have found something to fight over even without a garden," I say. "Mo and I fought a lot as kids. It's just something brothers and sister do."

"You're probably right."

We've been standing here for a while, and the interns have started heading back to the farmhouse with their yields. I slap at a mosquito that whines by my ear, but I don't want to leave.

"Where's your sister now?" I ask.

"She's stationed in San Diego right now—I told you she's a naval officer, right?"

I nod. I can hear the pride in his voice.

"After I enlisted in the army, she decided she wanted to

195

try military life. She joined ROTC at her school and picked the navy, probably just to spite me."

Seeing my blank look, he clarifies. "They're big football rivals."

"Come on, beautiful," Trudy calls out from the edge of the field. "Let's break. Time for grub."

We take our baskets to a large table under an overhang near the interns' quarters by the fields where a couple of them are bundling the greens. They wave off our offers to help. Empty harvest boxes are stacked in towers on the porch. The bundled collard greens will join portions of lettuce, peas, squash, bok choy and cabbage that'll be handed out at the Saturday market for the CSA members. Anything left over after the boxes are filled will be sold.

"We're good," says one with long hair and a shell-and-hemp necklace. She looks approvingly at Emmett's inked arms, and I feel a ridiculous stab of jealousy. "We're almost done."

"Finished," I correct her under my breath. Emmett, who hears me, stifles a laugh.

He takes my hand, which is hot and grimy despite the gardening gloves I borrowed. I try to hide my surprise and act like holding hands with him is normal. Like my jealousy is warranted. Maybe he didn't like her appraising look either. The thought pleases me no end.

We head off to the outdoor sink and scrub our hands. I splash cold water on my face, sighing with pleasure, and feel the drops slide down my neck, disappearing under my tank. When I open my eyes, eyelashes clumped with water, I catch an odd, hungry look in Emmett's eyes. But as soon as he realizes I see him, he settles his features into their usual calm, impassive lines and I wonder what I saw there.

"Come on, beautiful," he says, using Trudy's nickname for me and making me blush. "Let's eat. I'm starving."

The vegetarian dinner, served outside under Japanese lanterns lit with flickering candles, is the perfect ending to what has so unexpectedly turned into a lovely evening.

The interns, quirky and idealistic, with their sunburned noses and callused hands, are easy to talk to. The food, much of it picked that day at the farm, is light and delicious, and for once my stomach doesn't shriek in protest as it fills. There's roasted corn on the cob, tomato-and-green-bean salad, berries with sweet cream and, since one of the interns used to work at a bakery, fresh-baked bread and oatmeal raisin cookies for dessert.

Even though I'm the one who called Trudy in the first place, even though her invitation may have sprung from pity or the ulterior motive of involving another picker in the harvest, being here at dinner with Emmett by my side and this group of kind, gentle souls feels like a gift.

The farm is far away from the city's lights, and as night descends, the surrounding land turns from its familiar darkness to a pitch black I'm not used to. The lanterns invest the picnic with an otherworldly glow. For the duration of the evening, I feel removed from all my problems. My fears, my diagnosis and the troubles waiting for me fade, and I feel so light and free I could fly.

I'm learning to notice these gifts when I receive them, and I send a little thank-you up to the sky, heavily freckled with stars.

XVIII.

WHEN IT COMES TIME for my weekly phone calls to my parents, I again fight the urge to tell them about my diagnosis. I want to, since it's what both of them would want me to do and because they're my parents. They're the ones I'm supposed to go to when bad things happen in life. I want them to make my illness go away, or at least to make me feel better about it. But there's nothing they can do, and out of misplaced worry, they might insist I come back home. That would be disastrous. Instead of telling them anything important, I promise to mail them copies of the article on Trudy and Hank. I'm proud of my piece, although once it was published, I noticed some wording I wished I could change.

After the night at the farm, it feels like maybe God is paying attention . . . like maybe He is trying to help me. I wonder again if I'm right about being punished. Maybe Crohn's really has nothing to do with Tabitha or Jason. Regardless, I can't stop my mission now. So during my phone calls, I continue to lie.

When my dad asks if I'm okay, I tell him I'm fine, just tired from working hard (which he approves of). I tell my mother I've been feeling a little sick with a nasty stomach bug, and promise to drink plenty of tea and eat only dry toast and applesauce.

They both believe me, which is a relief but which saddens me as well. It shouldn't be that easy to lie, to be so convincing.

I guess I have a bit of Mo in me after all.

As the days go by, I try to crack through Jason's defenses. He is a surly and reluctant assistant, rolling his eyes when I ask him to make copies, grunting when I ask him for his opinion. And even though he occasionally volunteers an unprompted sentence or two—even though his face is no longer actively hostile, just sort of neutral and blank—I can tell I'm not winning. I insist he come with me on assignments, I try to schedule interviews so he can attend. I have him write headlines, which he doesn't enjoy, and let him take photos, which he seems to like.

Whatever or whoever it is I'm fighting Jason for, whatever it is I'm supposed to save him from, I'm not really any closer than before.

I debate telling all this to Mo. I still can't get over how well he and Jason hit it off that one afternoon at the coffee shop. If anyone had the key to unlock Jason, it would be my brother. But I don't. Mo never did find a job in town, and yet he's always gone. Always busy, always out late. And never short of money.

That's the part I can't figure out. Mo could make friends with a tree, so it doesn't surprise me he found people to hang out with. But where did he get the money for Chinese take-out, for the stacks of pizza boxes I find crammed into the trash can, for a double latte and muffin at the coffee shop every morning? He has weird new clothes that look ridiculous on him—long, baggy shorts he wears sagging below the waist-band of his boxers. He reeks of cigarette smoke even though he's never smoked before. He should be broke. He should be on a strict diet of ramen noodles and mooching free coffee at the office, which was what I fully expected when he first came to visit.

Perhaps I was stupid to think he had come to me of his own volition. Naïve to have any doubt about what was really going on or to imagine that giving him space would get him to open up. In hindsight, I should have known. The signs were there, but it wasn't anything I wanted to see.

I don't know how much longer I would have continued with my self-deception. In retrospect, I have to wonder if what finally and irrevocably ripped the blinders from my eyes wasn't another sort of divine intervention.

If it was, it was a cruel bit of kindness.

XIX.

I **NEVER INTENDED** to snoop through any of Jason's things. I believed we would grow to trust each other—I didn't kid myself that we'd be friends—and for him to trust me, I needed to trust him.

But after Jason's transfer (or demotion, depending how you look at it) to becoming my assistant, he uses my desk. My computer. My drawers.

So I never actually decide to snoop, but while cleaning out some clutter, I find Jason's journal under a pile of loose notes and flyers at the bottom of my drawer. Feeling my heart quicken, I carefully pull it out and glance around to see if anyone noticed. No one's paying the slightest attention to me, and so, with the notebook carefully balanced on my lap, I open it and take a peek at Jason's private work.

As I flip through the pencil-smudged pages, I quickly

realize this is not a random sketch pad, it's a graphic novel. The drawings are not bad, and I begin to think maybe Jason has some talent after all. Maybe he's not some hopeless, mediocre bag of crappy attitude and inferiority.

This makes me ridiculously happy. Of course I can't let him know I ever saw his drawings, but just knowing Jason has a talent, even a secret one, makes me like him better. I can't figure out why he doesn't let anyone see his sketches, but as I page through them, I marvel at certain expressions he's captured with just a few strokes of his pencil.

But then, as I read the thought bubbles—dialogue and narration written in oddly familiar block letters—my happiness drains away.

The drawings might be great, but the story . . . the story is horrifying. I turn the pages faster and faster as the plot evolves. It's about a boy who sneaks guns into an elite private school. With malicious glee, he executes the football team, then maims and taunts the cheerleaders as they beg for their lives. The drawings here are darker, as if Jason leaned heavier on his pencil, reveling in the spurting blood, the exploding eyeballs and the oozing brain matter of the once perfect and beautiful students.

I feel sick and dirty, but that's not the worst. I might have been able to convince myself this was only fantasy, a harmless escape for a miserable boy. But the handwriting—that familiar print—is not Jason's writing. It isn't Jason's plotline.

It's Mo's.

XX.

"WE NEED TO TALK."

"Not tonight," Mo says as he steps into the apartment, sounding like a weary husband confronted by a nagging wife.

I've been sitting at the kitchen table for five hours, waiting, waiting for him to come home, scared to leave and miss him, with my anger, terror and frustration simmering under pressure as the clock on the wall ticks. Betrayed, I keep thinking. I've been betrayed. It's one, and the early morning hour lends this meeting an eerie sense of unreality.

"No," I say, my voice shaking with rage. "Tonight. Now."

I'm so angry that I'm not tired. But I should have remembered that any show of temper always sparks Mo's.

"Back off, Miriam," he snaps.

I rise from my seat, my back sore from sitting for so long,

my stomach sour and cramping, and pound my fist down on the table. Harder than I mean to—the blow sounds like a gunshot and causes my glass of water to wobble, then topple and roll off the table. It explodes as it hits the tile, sending shards of glass skittering across the floor.

We stand there for a moment, frozen by the sudden violence.

"Well done," Mo finally says. But, stepping carefully between the pieces, he heads to where I keep the broom—something I'm surprised he knows.

I'm in my bare feet, so I stay put and watch as he carefully sweeps the glittering pieces into a small pile.

"I'll need to mop the floor now," I say, a bit petulantly. As if he's the one who broke the glass, not me. "The broom'll never get all the little pieces up." I sit and pull my bare feet up to the chair, hugging my legs to keep out of the way.

Mo doesn't answer, just keeps sweeping methodically, getting into corners, and eventually his pile is as much dust and crumbs as it is broken glass. I'm not much of a housekeeper.

He scoops it all up in a dustpan and pours it into the trash can. It tinkles as it drops.

"Now," he sighs, like the parent of an unruly teenager. "What was so fucking important?"

I'm momentarily struck dumb. The combination of his unusual thoughtfulness with the broom and the profanity throws me. For a moment, I feel like I'm the one who's done something wrong.

But the feeling doesn't last.

I pull the notebook out of the bag I've slung on the back

of the chair and place it on the table. We both stare at it as if I've produced a live snake, which in a way I have.

Mo's eyes shift from the notebook to me to the door.

"Don't even think about it," I say, my voice low and tight. "We're talking about this now."

I see him thinking, eyes flicking around, looking for the right way to spin this, but I shake my head to let him know there's no point in denying his part in this. His shoulders relax a bit, and I know he's chosen what to say. I'm pretty sure it isn't the truth.

"Isn't it a trip," he says. "Don't tell me you didn't laugh."

"Don't do this," I say.

"What? You didn't take all this seriously, did you?" He fakes incredulity. "Miriam," he says. "Come on, don't be a moron. We were just playing around. We have another notebook going where we're fighting space aliens who take over all the politicians in the country. Is that real too? Are you going to call NASA? The *National Enquirer?*"

"You're lying."

He puffs up with mock indignation. "I'm not."

Hugging my legs tighter, feeling cold and sick, I keep pushing.

"The only thing I'm wondering about is whether this was all your idea or if Jason contributed anything besides drawing the pictures."

His expression hardens into hostility.

"You think he likes going to that school? Let me guess. 'It's a great opportunity for someone like him,' right?" His tone mocks every adult sentiment we've ever been subjected to.

"I didn't say that," I say defensively. "I just want to know how much he hates it. Enough to bring a gun to school? Enough to shoot the students?"

I see Mo trying to rein in his emotions. He tries for flippancy again. "Look, it's better to just deal with how it feels to go to a fucked-up school like that. Better to get out how it really does suck to be surrounded by preppy freaks all day who think you're not fit to shine their shoes when in reality you're a hundred times better than they could ever be."

"Who are we talking about here?" I ask. "Jason or you?"

Mo's lips whiten as he presses them tightly together. "He's a really good illustrator," he finally says. "We're going to publish the story when we're done."

I'm at a loss for words. To think this has been going on for so long right in front of me. No wonder God is punishing me in His disgust. I cannot believe I've been so blind, and I cannot believe Mo has done this to me.

"Mo, did you make him do this? Is this your idea? All this time that you've been gone, you've been hanging out with Jason? You've been filling his head with all this . . . ?" Words fail me.

"She wants him to be a freaking U.S. senator, if you can believe it. I mean, what the hell chance does Jason ever have of becoming a senator?" he snorts. "She won't quit, though. Won't see what he's like, what's possible for him. And that fucking school she's sending him to . . ." Mo starts pacing around the kitchen, hands deep in his pockets, some nameless emotion shimmering off him. "You have any idea what it's like there? The Alpine Club flies to Switzerland to go skiing in the

Alps over spring break. The Polo Club expects members to have their own horses. And Jason's mom is bankrupting them just to pay for tuition. So what the fuck is he supposed to do? Everyone can tell from the minute they meet him that he doesn't belong there, and those assholes never let him forget it. He doesn't have a single friend in that entire school. This year's almost over, which means he's got two years left in that hellhole. Two years with his mother constantly asking him about his grades and why he isn't hanging out with this person's son or going out with that person's daughter when he doesn't even stand a chance. When no one will give him a chance.

"Worst part is, no one at school knows his mom's a mailman, mailwoman, whatever. And her route is right through Belleair Bluffs—where, like, eighty-five percent of the student body lives. It's, like, what's worse? The fact that none of them ever noticed their mailperson, or waiting for them to finally make the connection?"

"There's nothing wrong with being a mailman," I say quietly.

"Are you blind?" Mo snarls. "Their parents are producers and country music stars; they're millionaires. A couple of big-name musicians send their kids to school in a chauffeured limo. There's a senator who sometimes drops his kids off in a helicopter. So no, there's nothing fucking wrong with being a mailman. But it's a crime at Warfield."

I take a deep breath, ready to get a word in, but Mo's not finished with his rant and steamrolls right over me.

"You remember our freshman year at Breakman, don't you?" he demands.

Breakman was the elite private high school in our town. A few years after the divorce, my parents got the brilliant idea that sending us to a small, "nurturing yet structured" school was the best thing for us. It was a complete disaster. Mo and I didn't fit in; didn't have the right clothes, the right look. Most of the students had been together since preschool, always attending expensive, exclusive schools. They knew each other, slept with each other, got high together, covered up for each other, and were absolutely not interested in two half-Jewish bourgeois teenagers in the middle of their "awkward" stage. For me it meant eating lunch alone, occasional giggles behind my back and either eye-rolling or a condescending excuse at my tentative attempts to make friends.

For Mo it meant serious hazing on the track team by the seniors.

Of course I remember Breakman.

Two months into the school year, Mo was left in the back of the school van after a track meet, hands and ankles duct-taped together, pants and underwear pulled down to his ankles. He was left there for three hours before the driver found him.

My parents, united in their insane fury, descended on the principal. I don't know what went on behind closed doors, but several students "graduated early," Mo received a four-year college tuition scholarship courtesy of the school board and the next week we were attending the local public high school.

We never talked about Breakman again.

For Mo to bring it up now means that he's empathizing with Jason more than I ever imagined. Even if the plot of the story was Jason's idea in the first place, Mo, in the grip of some terrible flashback, is only adding fuel to the fire with his zealous approval.

I have time to think this in the quick moment before he looks me in the eye. I keep my face carefully blank. Who's the driving force behind his sudden bitterness, the need for vengeance? Is he being played, manipulated by the master of the game? Is this free will?

"You know Jason's taking this seriously," I say. "It's not a game to him. It's dangerous to egg him on like that. He's going to snap, and he's going to kill a lot of innocent people."

Instead of feeling chastened or concerned, Mo grows even more defensive.

"How do you know they're 'innocent people'?" he demands. After catching the look of horror and disgust on my face, he softens his tone somewhat. "Look, Miriam, even if Jason had the guts to do something, which he doesn't, the worst that will happen is that he'll sneak a gun to school and not feel like a jerk for one day."

"This isn't you," I say, desperate to believe it, to convince him. "This wasn't your idea. You've been given a mission." I'm guessing this, but as I say it, I believe it.

"Maybe I was," he says. "But this isn't evil. This is helping Jason become a stronger person, someone who matters. You're not helping; with all your stupid errands and assignments, you're like another teacher, except you're only three years older than he is. Where do you get off telling him what to do?"

And now I know why I haven't made any headway with my new assistant.

"You've sabotaged me! You knew I was trying to help!"

"Miriam," Mo says, dripping with condescension. "You can't help."

Then he grabs his keys and walks out, slamming the door behind him.

That night, I'm sick again. I've also started running a low-grade fever, which makes me achy and clammy, alternating between shivers and sweats. The twisting pain in my belly keeps me up for what's left of the night. Once again, I'm struck by how much I hate this disease. How it strips me of any dignity. This is the worst part, the ugliest part, of a human body to break down. The contrast between my writhing, sweaty form and the perfect and cold celestial beauty of the angels couldn't be greater or clearer.

I am nothing but mud.

XXI.

AFTER A LONG, SLEEPLESS NIGHT, I know I'm ruined for work. I call Frank and tell him I'm sick.

"Again?" he asks, concern and annoyance warring in his voice. "I hear you saw Dr. Messa. I hope everything's all right."

My skin flushes hot and cold at the thought that what I'm going through is becoming common knowledge.

"It's not that," I say stiffly. "Just a bug, pretty contagious. I don't want to get anyone else sick. I'll do some work at home on my laptop." I used to be a bad liar, but I'm improving.

"Fine, fine." He is irked at being rebuffed, at not getting an inside scoop, even though it's nothing salacious, or even interesting. "See that you get well, and I'll see you tomorrow."

I hang up and then review my options. It's no use going to Jason; he's picked his confidant, and I'm not it. Anything I say will make things worse. In fact, I call Frank back and ask him to tell Jason not to come to the newsroom today. I don't want him there until I can slip the notebook back into the drawer. He can't know I found it.

I go to the kitchen and stare at the notebook again. It looks so innocuous. I don't open it.

I call Dr. Messa's office and leave a message with the nurse to tell him the medicine isn't working.

An hour later, as I head toward Emmett's shop, my cell phone rings.

"Ms. Abbot-Levy?"

"Speaking."

"This is Dr. Messa. I received your message."

"Hi," I say, surprised. "Thank you for calling."

"I'm concerned about your situation," he says, his soft voice serious. "I want you to come in tomorrow. I've told Megan to fit you in. We need to discuss our options."

I sit down on a bench by an antiques store until my heart settles down and I don't feel nauseous.

"Okay," I say weakly. "Thanks."

I know there are prayers for healing. But I have a feeling that God already knows what I'm going through. Mercy and pity are not on today's agenda.

I hang on while I'm transferred to Megan, who finds a slot for me. I'm to come in first thing in the morning.

I'm running out of time. My disease is worsening, and the school year is almost over. If Jason's going to do anything, it will be soon, while he's got Mo there cheering him on.

There's no point in going to the police—not with the

notebook as my only evidence. It would only serve to let Jason know I've been snooping, to make him cover his tracks that much more. I need to prevent that courtroom scene, I need to save Jason, and calling the cops wouldn't really do that.

As I continue walking toward Emmett's, I notice I'm sweating, my legs quivering from what should have been a leisurely stroll. My strength is fading. From reading other people's posts online, I know I don't have much time before I'm hospitalized.

I make it to Emmett's shop, push open the door and sag into the cool darkness.

Someone is getting a tattoo, the tattoo gun buzzing like a busy bee. After a sharp glance up at me, Emmett goes back to his work. I settle on a nearby chair and watch him.

It's a bit gruesome as the blood wells and he wipes it away with an automatic gesture, the disposable towel growing bloody as the tattooed skin grows more and more colorful.

This tattoo is of the Confederate flag, a pretty design until you stop and think what it stands for. And then you wonder what the hell is wrong with people.

When Emmett finishes, our Rebel friend, wearing a faded T-shirt with the sleeves ripped off, goes over to the mirror and inspects his new tattoo. As Emmett cleans up his station, the man gives a low whistle of approval.

"You like it?" Emmett asks.

"It's just like I pictured it. You're a freaking artist."

Emmett nods slightly at the praise. He's drawn the flag flapping, the familiar X of stars nearly obscured and the ends

213

tattered, as if it's been buffeted by a stiff wind for a long time. There are two ways to read this tattoo: either with pride that the flag is still there or with relief that it's fading away. It's clear how the redneck interprets it: he looks at his triceps with gleeful delight. I wonder what Emmett was thinking as he inked it. He never struck me as a bigot. Only a businessman who does what people ask for.

Rebel pays and leaves and Emmett turns his full attention to me.

"You look like shit," he says. "Everything okay?"

I think about that for a moment.

When I don't answer, he says, "I guess not."

I chew on a nail, trying to decide what to say.

Emmett takes a look at his calendar and, after rubbing a hand across his bald head, shrugs, almost to himself.

"This calls for a drink," he says. He leans over the counter and grabs his keys and wallet. "Come on, my treat."

"The shop . . . ," I say halfheartedly.

"It's quiet today."

"You always say that," I remind him.

He smiles. "They're all quiet," he says, and holds out a hand for me to take. I look at his intimidating tats, his kind eyes, and then place my hand in his.

"Okay," I say. "Thanks."

Emmett doesn't drive into town like I expected him to. We cruise past Main Street and onto the hilly, scenic roads of the countryside. There's something relaxing about the rolling green hills, dotted with grazing horses and cows. It's even nicer riding in his clean car than it was in the back of the truck. The windows are strategically down to let in the early summer breeze, and I actually calm down from last night's upheaval.

We're halfway to Nashville when he turns into an unfamiliar state park and pulls into an overlook parking lot. We're the only car there.

"I thought we were going for a drink," I say.

He fishes around under the seat until he finds what he's looking for and, with a flourish, produces a half-empty water bottle. "A drink," he says, and hands it to me. It's warm from being in the car so long.

"Gross. How long has this been in here?"

"Less than a couple of weeks," he assures me. "Nothing but the best for you."

"Gee, thanks."

We share a smile, the mood lighter than it was at the shop.

"Want to take a look?" he asks, pointing at the view over the low stone wall that we're parked against.

I nod and we get out. There's a soft breeze that feels like a caress, and the beautiful view stretches out from here to forever. Everything looks like a miniature set: tiny houses and farms; cute, diminutive trees and little roads that wind between hills—a perfect little Pleasantville. There's just the very start of summer flowers: a few precocious black-eyed Susans and purple echinacea standing out amidst all the green.

"Doesn't even seem real," Emmett says, echoing my thoughts. I can tell he comes here often. Nothing seems real from up here, not even my problems. The dichotomy of this ethereal loveliness and the ugliness of people is almost too great to comprehend. I don't know how God can stand it.

We sit down on the stone wall, legs dangling over the ledge, the ground at least a hundred feet beneath us and sloping down sharply to a valley far below.

After about a minute of silence, Emmett turns to me and cocks an eyebrow.

I still haven't decided how much to tell him, and to stall for time, I automatically take a sip from the bottle. The water tastes like plastic, and I spit it out with a cry of disgust.

"I can't believe I just did that," I say, wiping my mouth.

"I can't believe you did that either," he says gravely, but fighting a smile. "I would never drink something that nasty."

I punch at his shoulder, but gently. I don't want him to topple over the edge.

With the mood light again, I smile at him, and then, because it seems he won't mind, I lean against his side until I'm cradled against him. He feels solid, and I know it was silly to worry about knocking him off the wall. I have the feeling he could stay there for years, like a statue, if he wanted to.

"A bunch of bad news came in all together," I say, as if picking up in the middle of a conversation. "Sometimes it all seems to come at once and it's too much, you know? More than I can fix."

"Like what?" he asks, a reporter wanting specifics.

"My meds aren't working like they should. I have a meeting tomorrow to discuss my options," I say, disgust dripping from my voice. "Frank's not happy with all the work I'm missing. If I give him the gory details, he'll get off my back, but I don't want to become the Friday feature. That man lives on gossip, grits and biscuits."

"Sounds like a country music song."

I snort.

I'm skirting the big problem, but even here, in this idyllic setting, it's hard to find the words. "And then, you remember my pet project, Jason the jerk?"

He nods.

"It's bad." I pause. "I found something of his, and I'm very concerned he's going to do something . . ." My voice trails off. Somewhere, hidden in some tree, a bird trills.

Emmett waits for me to continue. When I don't, he prods me: "And by 'something,' I assume you mean something bad."

I nod.

"Something very bad?"

I nod again.

"Something like robbing a bank?"

"Worse, if you can believe it. And . . ." I rub a hand across my face hard, thinking quickly how much I should and shouldn't reveal. "It's complicated. My brother's hanging out with him, and somehow they're egging each other on. And even though Mo thinks it's just a game—at least I think he thinks that—I have a very bad feeling that Jason's taking this seriously."

"You've talked to Mo?"

I nod silently.

"Didn't do much good, huh?"

"Clearly. I've been up all night, and I don't know what to do."

He sighs. "Well then, you need to go to the police with what you've found, Miriam."

He sees the look on my face.

"It's not like I think it's a great option. But it's your only one if you really think this thing, this disaster, is actually going to happen. If you don't get them involved and then this comes to pass, you'll always blame yourself."

"But I—I'm supposed to *help* Jason." I'm nearly crying with frustration and fear.

"Maybe stopping him is the best you can do for him." Emmett's voice is implacable, and not the least bit sympathetic. I don't know if that is because he's indifferent to Jason's plight or because he's lost patience with my one-track mind.

I want to tell him more. I want to tell him everything. He's so unflappable and practical. He would have good advice, assuming he believed me and didn't try to commit me to the nearest insane asylum for delusions of grandeur. At least they don't burn crazy heretics these days. Just dope 'em up and lock 'em down.

But I don't tell him. It's no use. It's too big a stretch of the imagination to think he could believe me, but even if he did, it would put him in a terrible position. This is Prometheus's burden. I can't set it down; I can't pass it on.

So I nod and say I'll think about it.

Emmett glances at me sharply, something dull in my tone

probably tipping him off that I've given up on getting through to him.

He looks a bit grim and then nods, almost to himself.

"You hungry?" he asks.

I make a face. "Nothing much agrees with me lately."

"I know a great place," he says gently. "Give it a try."

We go to a little French café in the artsy section of Nashville near Vanderbilt University, and Emmett orders us chicken soup and a crusty baguette. I'm charmed by this part of town, which I haven't been to before. It's full of students and weird boutiques selling handmade clothes for too much money. The soup stays down, and with so many cafés around, there are plenty of public restrooms, a fact that helps me enjoy myself as we stroll. I've learned never to let myself get too far away from a potty safe house.

On the drive back to town, we pass a church billboard proclaiming HE DOESN'T PROMISE AN EASY RIDE, ONLY A SAFE LANDING.

I close my eyes and spend the rest of the ride in silent darkness.

I feel Emmett's hand on my leg a little above the knee, on the skin exposed by my shorts. The warm weight is comforting. Without opening my eyes, I place my hand over his. He turns his hand and curls his fingers around mine. He doesn't squeeze or press my fingers. He just holds my hand, and I hold his until we make it back to town.

XXII.

WHEN MO COMES HOME THAT EVENING, I can tell by the set of his shoulders that he's expecting another fight. I don't want to fight, but I know he's my only chance to succeed with Jason.

I've made brownies, a pathetic offering that I hope will bring him to the table and keep this talk civil. As he catches the scent of warm chocolate, I see his posture relax just a bit.

"I've added peanut butter chips," I coax.

He rolls his eyes but comes to the kitchen table, sitting down warily.

"Eat," I say. "They're still warm."

So he sits and we eat together. I wait until he has a mouthful of brownies before I start to talk.

"Mo," I say. "I don't want to fight."

He nods but doesn't say anything, his face set in hard lines incongruous with his full mouth and the dark crumbs on his lips.

"You're my brother. I love you."

His face softens at my tone and he reaches out to touch my hand.

"Miriam, sis, you know I love you." Mo's eyes are shining; his face, so similar to mine, so familiar, beseeches me to trust him.

"I know you love me, Mo," I say, because what else can I tell him? He does love me. But that doesn't mean his love is pure. And it doesn't mean he hasn't hurt me.

I always forgive him. For the slights, for the tricks he played on me, for embarrassing me in front of my friends and laughing about me in front of his. Because at the end of the day, we're twins. I know why he does the things he does. I know him better than anyone else and he knows me. I've always felt that if I turned my back on him, he would be lost. Forever.

Then, with blinding clarity, I suddenly realize something I should have seen from the beginning: *the angels carried an image of Mo's face as well.* I'm stunned it hasn't occurred to me before. Jason and the students at Warfield aren't my only mission. I cannot believe I didn't see that my brother needs me as much as Jason does. The thought has me shaking with excitement. This isn't just about Jason, that hostile, defensive and surly boy I have nothing in common with. It's as much about Mo as it is about Jason. I feel a surge of energy and resolve at the thought. I may have fumbled with Tabitha. I might fail with Jason. But not with Mo. I will not let the devil have him. Because he's mine.

"Mo," I say, gathering my racing thoughts, struggling to control my voice. "This is important. This is more important than anything we've ever done. You know that."

I try to see if I'm getting through to him.

"This isn't a game." My voice cracks. "It's the angels and the devil fighting over this." *Over you*, I want to say but I don't. "How can you help Satan? How can you do that? It's a choice you make; it's not fate. And if you can't bring yourself to defy him completely, then please just don't *help* him."

"At least I'm talking to the man in charge; you're just dealing with some underlings," he taunts.

"That's because God is greater than the devil," I shoot back. "He can delegate this; Satan can't." Mo's face changes again, closes to me. In my sudden excitement, I haven't planned my strategy very well.

"Screw you!" he says. "How do you know that I'm on the devil's side?" I see the mulish, bitter look on his face. "Why do you assume that you're on God's side? You're blind. It's your arrogance and your pride. It's so typical. Little sister, you're in over your head."

"I'm trying to stop a *killing*," I say. "How can you possibly think doing anything else is right?" I can't pull back, not now that I understand the bigger picture. I know it's the wrong thing to do, but I just can't stop the words from tumbling out. "I've had more visits," I babble quickly. "Angels and visions. This is real. This is important."

Mo clenches his teeth and I see a muscle twitching on the side of his jaw. This isn't going the way I want, I think in sudden panic.

"Mo, please." I reach out my hand and he smacks it away. We both look shocked for a moment. My hand is red and stinging. I clutch it to my chest. He looks unhappy and scared, but before I can say anything, he pushes his chair back, scraping it loudly, and walks away.

"You're my brother!" I shout after him. "Come back!"

But his steps never falter and he doesn't look back.

XXIII.

THE NEXT DAY I HAVE MY APPOINTMENT with Dr. Messa, and I arrive in the waiting room heavy with a dull sense of dread.

The nurse who calls me in recognizes me and says hi with the warm friendliness reserved for repeat customers, a category I'm not pleased to be part of.

After a twenty-minute wait in the examination room, where I grow more and more cold and scared, Dr. Messa walks in with a professional smile on his face. We shake hands, his warm and dry, mine damp and frozen. Then he sits down on a small rolling stool and flips through my file. The smile fades as he scans the notes, and he sets the file down on the narrow counter next to him and gravely makes eye contact.

"So the Asacol isn't working," he says.

"No," I say softly.

"Bowel movements?"

I squirm, talking about this. I hate it. It's private; it should stay that way. But instead I try to match his matter-of-fact tone.

"I've lost count how many times I go a day. And I have a low-grade fever, off and on."

He nods.

"Well, Miriam, we have several options." He begins to explain that there's a pyramid of medication. I've been on the lowest rung, but I'm about to be promoted. As one climbs this pyramid, the medication grows more powerful, which means there's a greater likelihood that it'll suppress the disease but also a greater likelihood that my body will reject it or that I will experience serious side effects. Chronic nausea. Shingles. Cancer.

Should climbing this pyramid fail to help, either because the medication doesn't suppress the disease or because the side effects are too strong, then we're left with surgery.

"It's not the end of the world," he says, noting that I look pale. "Here, let me show you." On the thin, crinkly paper that covers the examination table, Dr. Messa begins to sketch a rough model of the colon.

"The most drastic option is a complete removal of the diseased colon." Drawing an X, he says, "This is where the surgeon cuts the colon and removes it. Then he pulls the ileum though the abdominal wall." He continues sketching quickly, the drawing crude but very illustrative. He keeps talking, and my face grows hot and then prickly with clammy heat. I feel woozy, and his voice grows distant. My sight shrinks to a narrow tunnel and then . . . winks out.

I come to on the examination table, lying right on top of the horrid sketch.

"Are you okay, dear?" the nurse asks. I don't remember her coming in, but I suppose Dr. Messa called for help when he realized his audience had just passed out.

I blink a couple of times and then try to sit up. The nurse puts a hand on my shoulder, pressing me down.

"Just stay there a bit, until everything settles."

"I'm so sorry," I whisper, for some reason humiliated.

"It's okay; you've been through a lot. I hate it when we see patients your age going through this. Hard enough when you're thirty. But in a young girl like you, it breaks my heart."

Her feelings are sincere, but her pity makes me feel even worse.

I turn my head away from her and close my eyes. She takes the hint and shuts up. I really don't enjoy hearing that my situation is pathetic. After the staff scrounges up an orange soda, which they insist I drink, I'm allowed to get off the examination table. I keep my eyes averted so as not to see Dr. Messa's illustration.

When I check out, I see him. He looks sheepish and comes over to me. As he stands by my side, I realize we're basically the same height, and I'm not a tall girl. I never noticed how short he was. Maybe being the bearer of bad news makes you seem taller. I wonder about his personal life, about his childhood. He must have been teased in high school. He became a doctor, and now he helps people. Why do some people shrug off teenage misery while others don't?

Dr. Messa doesn't meet my eyes; he just pats me on the back a couple of times and says, "Don't worry, Miriam. It might not come to that. We'll take care of you. We'll lick this thing."

He means to be kind, so I just nod and don't say anything.

I return to the office, working mechanically. I write words I don't understand, have conversations I don't remember. I wait until I get back to my apartment before I start crying. But this time, the crying doesn't last long. My eyes are sore from crying so much, my soul tired.

Is this God's work? Another kick in the pants for always failing? I think back on Hank's musings on the nature of disease. Is it the devil trying to slow me down? If it is the devil, then why isn't God stopping him?

I log on to an online Bible, looking for answers, hoping for comfort. Random clicking leads me to Psalms, my favorite book of the Bible. I mean to click on Psalm 23, which seems appropriate, given the situation, but end up reading Psalm 51, my mother's favorite:

> *Surely I was sinful at birth,*
> *sinful from the time my mother conceived me.*
> *Surely you desire truth in the inner parts;*
> *you teach me wisdom in the inmost place.*
> *Cleanse me with hyssop, and I will be clean;*

wash me, and I will be whiter than snow.
Let me hear joy and gladness;
let the bones you have crushed rejoice.

This has me shuddering. I feel even lower than I did. Was I sinful at birth? Is God justified in His judgment of me, judgment of my failure? Perhaps He has given up on His attempts to teach me wisdom. I click to Psalm 91, which my father and I had discussed in the past. It is a bit more comforting:

Surely he will save you from the fowler's snare
and from the deadly pestilence.
He will cover you with his feathers,
and under his wings you will find refuge;
his faithfulness will be your shield and rampart.
You will not fear the terror of night,
nor the arrow that flies by day. . . .
No harm will befall you;
no disaster will come near your tent.
For he will command his angels concerning you
to guard you in all your ways.

I laugh hollowly at the irony of those last lines. Spare me the guardianship of angels. The air-conditioning clicks on and a cold wind blows down my neck. I shiver but don't rise. I reread the entire passage. There is something so compelling about the thought that God protects His beloved. Of course my mind wanders back to the dream at the ruins. The impossible voice promising shelter and safety. Is there any way that it could be real? Let's assume that His angels have been guarding me. That would mean that this whole intervention was for my benefit. At first the thought seems preposterous. This whole ordeal has been nothing but trouble for me, from the terrifying, blinding beginning to this current situation of illness and frustration. But as I continue to sit in front of the glowing screen, struggling with my thoughts, the simple, ancient verses fill my vision; they sink into my brain and I start to see things in a different light.

If I take the events of the past few months and filter them through the lens that I am not a victim, that no celestial being bears me ill will and that in fact this has all been for my well-being, then suddenly everything sharpens in focus and the picture before me bears little resemblance to the way I've seen things until now. Because suddenly I see that showing me people in need and granting me the opportunity to make a difference in someone's life is a gift, not an injury. I still think angels aren't my biggest fans, but perhaps the motive behind the cruelty was pure.

Because without a visit, would I ever have believed my brother's encounter? Would I even realize he needed a champion, that he needed me?

No. Of course the answer is no. I never would have believed he needed me, and when he confessed his encounters with the devil, I wouldn't have believed what he said.

It's a mind-altering epiphany.

Raphael's visit, the dream, the vision—these were a boon granted to me, and in my selfish, self-involved pity, I failed to see them for what they really were.

I sit back in my chair, stunned by the thought. A gift. Not a punishment. Not an unfair task, but rather a chance to achieve something truly important in life. I close my eyes and rest my head on the heels of my hands. How could I have misunderstood so badly? The late morning sun streams in between the blinds, casting lines across the carpet, the desk and my arms.

I realize something else. My disease can help me. It could be just the thing I need to get through to Mo. Whether God-given, devil-cursed or a biological fluke, without it I don't stand a chance.

In a daze, I scroll up to the passage I logged on for, meaning to read.

I have always found Psalm 23 beautiful. But now, as I walk through my own valley, my own shadow—if not of death, then at least of what seems like a desecration of my body—it's been hard to feel anything but abandoned, discarded, betrayed. As Psalm 23 appears and my face is bathed by the eerie blue glow of the screen, I read it again. Maybe a promise that no harm will befall me, that no disaster will come near me, is not a literal promise of good health. It's a state I can reach if my heart and my soul are ensconced in the shelter of faith. And knowing that I am not being punished, believing that I am loved, goes a long way toward that.

> *Surely goodness and love will follow me*
> *all the days of my life,*
> *and I will dwell in the house of the Lord*
> *forever.*

XXIV.

Mo is avoiding me, but now that I know what I have to do, that's easy to fix. I log off and text him to meet me at the Civil War ruins. I'd told him about it, and as far as I know, he hasn't made it there yet. I put a sketch of the hike on the kitchen table and then head off, leaving my cell phone conspicuously behind.

If he has no way to weasel out of it, he'll come. I'll give him until an hour before dark before calling it quits.

But I know my brother. He won't be able to resist checking out an off-the-beaten-track Civil War site. If he knows I'm there waiting for him, if he can't tell me no, he'll come.

The walk to the ruins is even more difficult than it was the last time. It's a hot, humid day, for one, and the moisture in the air seems to suck the breath right out of my chest. And I've grown weaker. My legs feel rubbery and my breath catches

231

as my heart flutters, trying hard to keep up. My fever is back, making the day feel like both a blazing scorcher and too cold. I stop to rest frequently, cursing under my breath as I do.

I make it to the site and sit down, leaning back against a mound in the shade. I could be leaning against a ruined barracks, a storage room or maybe even the latrines, though probably those would be farther away from the living quarters. I close my eyes and try to bring my racing heartbeat down to a more sustainable level.

It is two hours before Mo finds me. I'm tired, but calm. I've had enough time to arm myself for this battle. It's my last chance. And I know what's going to happen to me, to Mo, to Jason, if I fail. It's ironic that Mo himself gave me the weapons. Misdirection, charm, familial loyalty. I've had time to think about how to approach this situation, and I'm taking a page from his book, treading that fine line between cleverness and manipulation. After nineteen years, I know what makes him tick and I don't hesitate to use it.

Mo flashes a crooked smile my way.

"You tricky little bitch," he says. He is partly enchanted by the ruins, partly pissed off that I got him to come, and partly admiring that I cornered him. Mo has always had a healthy respect for a worthy adversary.

"If it makes you feel better," I say, because he's never called me a bitch before and because things are already going badly, "this is the last time I'm going to talk to you about this."

"About time," he says, his back to me as he sizes up the place. I give him a moment to admire it. He explores it, clambering over the mounds, walking the perimeter, poking around its nooks and crannies. I wait until he circles back to me, antsy and ready to go.

"I wanted to give you the rest of the story before you make your decision." I can tell by the set of his shoulders that he thinks this is all bullshit. That I'm about to spin some sort of guilt trip, some human-interest story to sway him.

"Will you just settle down for a second?" I ask.

"Miriam, you have been fucking with me and wasting my time—"

I stop the tirade. "You know the weight loss that started before I left school?"

He stops kicking at one of the mounds near me but doesn't say anything. His hands are buried deep in his pockets, his shoulders hunched forward. I notice absently that we're wearing the same colors today, something that hasn't happened since Mo came to Hamilton.

"And all the times I run to the bathroom? The fact that I always look like crap? The fact that I have no energy?"

"You're bulimic?" he asks jeeringly, kicking at a loose rock.

"No." I say it quietly but it gets through to him. He can tell from my voice I have bad news, and he tenses, waiting. I take a deep breath. "I have a disease. It took the doctors a while to diagnose me, but it's an autoimmune disease that has my own body attacking itself, cannibalizing my intestines and shredding them into a horrible bloody mess."

"God damn it, Miriam," Mo says. "If you're fucking with me again and this is some sort of trick . . ." His hand is out and curled into a fist, the muscles bunched tight in his arm.

His whole body is coiled, ready to attack. He looks like he wants to hit me.

"It's not a trick," I say, fighting a sudden urge to cry. "I have Crohn's disease." His fist uncurls, and some of the tension seeps out of his body. "I don't know if you know much about it. I'd never heard of it until I was diagnosed. Because it's an autoimmune disease and my own body for some reason has decided to attack my colon, the only thing to do is try and shut down part of my immune system." I pause. "That's a difficult thing to do. So far, it's not working."

"Shit, Miriam," he says. "Are you serious?" He rubs a hand across his face like he's trying to wake up.

"I haven't been dieting. The pounds just fall off. I'm scared if I keep losing weight like this, I'll disappear." I cover my face.

He squats down next to me and pulls my hands from my face. "Tell me," he says urgently. Mo holds my hand and we automatically clasp our hands in our secret hold, where our middle fingers curl inside both our palms, sharing the warm space we make. I hold on to that contact, take comfort from it, before going on.

"I know you're wondering what that has to do with anything, but think about it," I say, meeting his eyes, his pained expression. "It started after I botched my first mission. This is a disease that can be genetic, but we don't have anyone in the family with it. I'm not doing a great job with Jason. And in the meantime, I just get sicker. I've already lost fifteen pounds in two months; my joints ache; I have a constant low-grade fever. I can't sleep because of the cramping and the urgency. I'm tired all the time because my body is falling apart. And the thing is, if I can't get this flare-up under control soon"—my voice rises alarmingly—"they'll need to take out my colon." My throat closes; I can't get those ugly words out. "I'll be a nineteen-year-old with a colostomy bag. I—"

Mo doesn't let me say any more; he grabs me in a rough, hard hug, smothering my face, my words, in his chest. Then he pushes me back a bit to look at me.

"Why didn't you tell me?" The look on his face is anguished and intense. Worry, love and rage flash in his eyes so quickly it's hard to tell one from the other.

"How could I? How can I ever tell anyone?" I start crying in earnest. "You have to help me, Mo. If I fail God on this, He's going to punish me worse, I know it."

There's a part of me watching this scene, weighing its effect on Mo. Is he buying this? Is it over the top? For this to work, he can't have any doubts about whether this is God's punishment or a life-sucks coincidence outside the realm of my mission. And if it's the devil who's doing this to me, I certainly don't want Mo to know. It has to be black-and-white: God is punishing me for failing with Jason. Mo has to fully believe. That's the only way I can help them both.

"This is bullshit," Mo rages above my head, his hands digging protectively into my back. "I thought you were supposed to be on the good guys' side; what happened to fucking free will?"

"I don't know, Mo," I say, my eyes closed, my forehead resting against his chest. His heart beats hard and fast. "The rules have changed. Just contacting me and getting me to try to change people's minds—how is that not messing with free will? Don't think I haven't thought about this. Stopping Jason from going through with this nightmare—that's the only thing I can do. Please, Mo, please say you'll help me." My heart is pounding as fast and as hard as his. He cannot know this is as much about him as it is about Jason and me.

Mo—my brother, my twin, my night and shadow—kisses my hair softly.

"We'll take care of this," he says gruffly. "We'll fix this together."

I sag a little and start crying in relief. Big messy sobs of release. He's not going to the devil; I won't fail again.

I hope the angels are hearing this; I hope they're here, watching what love can do. I want them to scurry back to Him, the Almighty, bearing the news that Mo is not perfect but that he's mine. He loves me, and that has to count for something.

"It's okay, Miriam," Mo says softly, holding me tightly. "I love you best of all."

Take that, I say silently to those jealous, perfect and awesome seraphim. *Take that*.

After the tears and hugs finally end, I start telling him my ideas for the best way to stop Jason.

Mostly I talk and Mo listens. I've had a lot of time to think about this, to plan the best approach. The way I see it, if the two of us meet with Jason, then I could talk him out of it and Mo's presence would help bolster my argument. I don't want to get Mo into trouble. He hasn't told me much of his conversations with the demon, but in case he promised him something, I don't want Mo to break his word and end up double-crossing the devil—that would turn out badly. I also reluctantly realize that I don't trust Mo to be convincing. He'd try, but I know he doesn't believe in stopping Jason like I do, which is why I want to do the talking.

Even now, as I explain what I think Jason might say and the best response to it, Mo sits next to me, pulling up clumps of grass with a vacant sort of look on his face.

"Are you listening?" I ask.

He shoots me a look. But as I pick up where I left off, I can tell his thoughts are wandering. It either means that I'm boring him—always a possibility with my brother's short attention span—or that he's figuring something out, planning, plotting something that may have nothing to do with what we're talking about. Or everything.

"We'll go to his house tonight," I say. I love my brother, but I have to be realistic. "We can't waste any time."

We walk back to town together. Mo keeps glancing at me as he notices how slowly I walk.

"You look like Gramma Birdie, walking like that," he says.

I save my breath and give him the finger. It makes him laugh, but I can feel the worry pulsing off him. I wonder how much of it is for me and how much is for what will happen when the devil realizes his disciple isn't following orders. Then I feel a rush of shame at the thought. I'm worried for him too.

Neither one of us has said this out loud, but if my Crohn's disease is God playing dirty, hurting me for failing, what would the devil do to Mo? Even if I'm right in assuming that my disease has nothing to do with God, it's unlikely the devil would refrain from punishing a wayward minion. This haunts me. I wonder if by saving Mo, I've doomed him as well.

When we arrive back at my apartment, Mo is already jumping with excess energy. His muscles twitch like those of a horse plagued with flies. He's got all his tics going—he's chewing the side of the nail on his thumb, tapping his foot, drumming his fingers on the table in a quick, nervous beat. I can't stand being around that.

"I'm heading to the shower," I say. I'm sweaty and gross after the long walk, and I don't want BO to drive Jason away before I get a word in.

"That's cool," he says a bit distractedly, keeping up with a heavy metal band only he can hear.

By the time I'm dressed after my shower, Mo's gone.

There's a note written in Mo's blocky print with directions to Jason's house. My heart sinks when I read it. He says he promised to have dinner with some friends, so he'll meet me at Jason's house at seven.

Of course I'm suspicious and uneasy, but there's nothing I can do about it, and I decide that I have to trust Mo. Mo's never broken his word to me. Twisted it, bent it, dodged it, sure, but never flat-out broken it. His feelings for me at the ruins were real, and I know that he loves me. I let that assuage my misgivings as I practice what to say to Jason when I see him tonight.

Don't worry, I tell my invisible, judging angels. *He'll come through for me.*

XXV.

WHEN I ARRIVE AT JASON'S PLACE, a modest duplex in a tired complex close to the local paint factory, Mo's not there. I wait a few minutes, but when he doesn't show up, I wonder if this is his compromise. He won't help stop Jason, he'll just cease driving him on. It's better than nothing, and I don't blame Mo. He has his own demons to deal with, literally. I figure that as long as he's not actively helping the devil, God will find a way to forgive the work he's already accomplished on his behalf. Besides, like with any vice, it might take a while to fully disconnect. One step at a time.

I've already forgiven him as I jog up the front steps to Jason's home.

I knock on the paint-chipped door. Jason's visibly surprised when he opens it and sees me.

"Hey," I say. "Can I come in for a second?"

He stands still for a moment, blocking the way, and then, with a characteristic shrug and rolling of his eyes, he shuffles aside to let me in.

His place is dark, with a few low-wattage bulbs illuminating two sagging recliners in faded blue velour and a stained gray carpet. A pizza box, dirty cups and used napkins litter the coffee table, while a too loud television blasts out hard-core rap, the flickering screen full of nearly naked women gyrating near a hot tub.

"Is your mom home?"

"She's working."

It occurs to me she must have a second job to help pay for tuition.

"This will only take a minute." I glance over at the TV. With a stony face, Jason digs out the remote from the cushions of one of the recliners and flicks it off.

"Yeah?"

I take a deep breath, priming myself for the fight to come.

"I found this at work," I say, pulling out the notebook. "You're an incredible artist."

For a split second he stands amazed at the compliment. Then he realizes what I'm holding out to him, and the look vanishes, transmuting instantly into defensive rage.

"That's private, bitch," he says, snatching it out of my hand.

"That's the second time today I've been called that." I fight for the right tone. "I don't appreciate it. And you shouldn't have left something private in my desk if you didn't want me to find it." And I wonder about that. Perhaps he did want me, or someone, to find it. Perhaps he was looking for someone to stop him.

He clenches his teeth, and I see the tendons in his jaws popping. He's also clutching the notebook to his chest like a child with a blankie. He looks young but unpredictable. He looks dangerous.

"I can't say I liked the plotline much, but the illustrations were amazing." I talk quickly but calmly, trying to change the mood between us. "I was thinking, if you're interested, about seeing if Frank will let you do some illustrations for the columns instead of using stock photos. Or, if you wanted, maybe you could do a cartoon strip."

Jason glares at me and then spins away, stalking over to the crooked blinds on the window.

"Take your sweet charity and shove it," he says with his back to me. "No one wants to hear what I've got to say."

"It's not charity," I say. "And no one wants to hear what you've got to say because mostly you don't say anything."

He swivels to glare at me.

This isn't going exactly as I planned, but at least he's reacting with more than a grunt or two. And since being confrontational seems to draw him out, I let him have it.

"See, that's all you do. Glare. Roll your eyes. Sneer. It's a nice repertoire you've got, but you can't be too surprised people don't eat it up." It feels good to be blunt, to finally say what I've been thinking. I'm not scared of him anymore.

He seems kind of surprised by that, but quickly recovers.

"You don't know anything about me," he says, taking a menacing step toward me, pointing a finger at my chest. "So just take your skinny ass out of my house before I call the cops."

"Actually, I know more about you than you think."

"You talked to Frank, right? He told you he let me have the internship so that Principal Finely will owe him a big one, right? I'm just making sure that he earns the favor, that's all."

"That's not what I mean."

"Screw you. You don't know anything about me. Now get the hell out of my house."

"Will you sit down and shut up for a second?" I say, losing my temper. "I just need to tell you something and then I'll leave, okay? But I've come all this way, and let's be honest, it isn't because you're so much fun to be around. So sit!"

He sits on the edge of one of the recliners. I gingerly sit down on the other. It rocks a little, and I hold on to the armrests to keep my balance. The smell of stale pizza and cheap carpet deodorizer are making me queasy. I have one shot to convince him, and my nerves aren't helping my roiling stomach.

"What I'm about to tell you is really hard to believe. I hope it helps that you know I wouldn't be here if I didn't believe it." I pause for a second, take a deep breath and plunge in. "I saw you in a dream." My voice shakes a little as I say this, and my armpits are wet with sweat. "Before I ever met you, I saw you in a dream, and in my dream I'm supposed to keep you safe."

Jason's eyes flicker to and away from me; he shifts his weight to the back of the recliner.

"But after I had the dream, which was before I ever met you, I didn't know what I was supposed to do for you," I say, leaning forward. "Then, after I met you, you didn't seem to want or need any help. I was lost but I didn't know what to do. But then, once I found your notebook, I knew. And I know something else. If you do this, you will get caught and you will go to jail. For a long time. For the rest of your life." My hands dig into the worn upholstery. "I saw it all, Jason. I promise I'm telling the truth."

He seems to be listening to me, but at the mention of the notebook his eyes narrow and I know he doesn't believe me. I swallow back the tears stinging my eyes and clogging my throat. Knowing I have no other choice, I tell him about Tabitha.

It doesn't take long to tell, my pathetic tale of failure and doubt. I simplify things and say it was another dream, a terrifying one. I tell him how I met Tabitha and still, idiotically, hesitated. I tell him about that afternoon, the brewing storm, my growing panic. And then of the botched rescue, the exploding building and Tabitha permanently disfigured, all because of me.

"I heard about that girl," he says quietly. I had forgotten that the incident made national news. For a split second I'm grateful to the obnoxious, unkind media for giving me credibility with Jason.

"I can't fail again. My dreams are real. Maybe it's God trying to tell me something." I can almost hear the angels snickering. I ignore that and continue. "This is about you," I say, "but as awful as this sounds, it's just as much about me. I'm already paying the price for failing once." I don't go into the details. "I can't fail again. You can save both of us." I'm trying to give him power, to share the gift for making a difference.

Our eyes meet. For the first time, Jason looks me straight in the eyes. His are a pale golden brown that's almost the color of caramel, with thick, dark lashes. It makes me sad that I never noticed.

"I know you're angry, Jason," I say. "You have every right to be. But high school sucks for a lot of people. The point is that you get through it and then leave it all behind. You go to college somewhere where there are people who you like. People who don't live for money or clothes or status. With your talent, you could easily get into an art school."

"My mom—" he begins.

"It doesn't matter what your mom plans for you," I say fiercely. "It's not up to her. After high school you move out; you're an adult and you make your own decisions. I understand she has dreams for you. Big dreams. But it doesn't matter. You can't live the life she always wanted." He turns his head away. "Tell her that *she* needs to run for office. Tell her you'll vote for her." He gives a watery chuckle.

"I mean it, Jason," I say. I feel a rising excitement. He wipes his eyes roughly and I know I'm connecting. He's listening. This is going to work. The words come out so easily, the right words. I'm full of inspired happiness. "You've got to start dreaming big. Your own dreams. You've got talent to spare. Now you need a little inspiration."

He breathes heavily. He looks at me, a look of suspicion that's holding back the floodgates of hope. It makes my heart catch. He swipes at his nose, and then, just as he's about to say something, there's pounding on the door. We both jump and turn in surprise. A deep voice shouts: "POLICE!! POLICE! OPEN UP!" We gape at each other and stand up, but apparently not fast enough. Police break down the door. Three of them rush in, shouting: "POLICE! HANDS UP IN THE AIR! HANDS UP IN THE AIR! GET DOWN ON THE GROUND! DOWN ON THE FUCKING GROUND! GET DOWN!!!"

I'm frozen in utter shock, and Jason lurches, as if to run away. Weapons drawn and pointed, the police come charging at us. They shove us to the floor. I sprawl facedown on the grimy carpet. I feel a knee between my shoulder blades and a rough voice asking me something. With my face mashed flat, I'm not sure what he's asking for, but suddenly one of my arms is bent behind my back and cold metal cinches my wrist. Just as I think of moving my other arm, it's yanked behind me and fastened in the handcuffs too. Hard, impersonal hands touch me everywhere, and seconds later I hear the same rough voice say, "Girl's clear."

"Guy's clear too," a different voice says.

With my head cocked, I see Jason pulled up, his arms behind his back in cuffs. Then it's my turn to be dragged up, like fish yanked from water.

A policeman wearing rubber gloves emerges from the back of the duplex, carrying two semiautomatic rifles. I stand in the bustling room, dumbfounded by how quickly everything is unraveling. Thinking is like swimming through mud. Stupid with shock, I cannot figure out how my success has been snatched away.

"Look what I found under the bed," the policeman crows.

Another man, in plain clothes, has already picked up the notebook and is flipping through it.

"It's all here," he says as he scans the pages. "Sick bastard."

Someone asks me my name, and numbly I give it. He writes it down, and asks for my telephone number and address. With a growing sense of indignation, I realize one of them has opened my wallet and is flipping through my credit cards, studying my driver's license.

Jason is already being led away, and I can hear the plain-clothes guy reading him his rights. Then someone is standing in front of me.

"You have the right to remain silent. If you give up that right, anything you say can and will be used against you in a court of law. You have the right to an attorney. . . ." I stop paying attention. I don't need an attorney. I need a miracle.

There are several men in the living room, taking photographs, searching the apartment. The adrenaline rush that propelled them through the door has dissipated. It's business as usual now, and I can't stand it.

My mind suddenly explodes into real time. The meaning of everything that just happened, of everything that will happen, of my failure, is sharply in focus.

"He changed his mind!" I shout at them. "He wasn't going to do it."

The men glance at me for a second, then continue what they were doing.

"He wasn't going to do it." My voice cracks.

"Let's go for a little ride," says the one who cuffed me as he grabs an elbow, leading me out.

My eyes fill with tears that quickly spill over. I try to think of something to say, something to get through to them. But Jason's already gone, and these men don't want to hear what I have to say. Less than five minutes ago, Jason was on the cusp of saving himself. Now no one can save him. Who called the police? Why are they here?

I can't swipe at the tears or my running nose, so tears and snot course down my face unchecked as I'm escorted to one of the police cars that are piled onto the grass in front of the apartment complex. The many blue and red lights flash and strobe, painting the buildings in garish colors. Several neighbors have opened their doors to see the action. Feeling utterly small and defeated, I duck into the sedan, falling to my side on the vinyl seat since I can't catch myself. As the cruiser pulls away, I notice that the door to Jason's apartment is wide open. I can see the police still there, going through drawers, poking into every little thing. I don't know if they broke the door so badly it won't close or if no one bothered to shut it after walking Jason to the police car.

It's not long before I'm sitting in an interrogation room, facing an image of myself in what must be a two-way mirror. I've seen enough television to know that everything I say is recorded and everything I do is being watched. I figure that Jason must be in another room. I hope that he's not hurt; I know he can't be okay.

A friendly-looking cop comes in, sipping coffee from a

Styrofoam cup. The smell fills the room and reminds me of the newspaper's break room. When he takes off my handcuffs, I expect that he'll tell me I can go, but instead he walks around the table, pulls up a seat, then opens a folder and glances through it.

He looks like someone's dad, like a Little League coach. But as he begins talking, calmly and politely, his questions send a shiver of fear down my spine. What was I doing at Jason's? How do I know him? How was I planning to help him? Why did I want to hurt the students at Warfield?

The line of questioning tells me that as far as the police are concerned, I am as much involved as Jason.

"I work at the paper; Jason's my assistant," I say. "I found the notebook in my office desk, and I thought if I talked to him, I could change his mind."

The cop has a polite look of disbelief, like I just told him about a great deal on a used car. "Oh, so Jason told you he changed his mind, that he'd given up on the whole idea?"

"If you guys hadn't barged in when you did," I say, growing angry, "then he would have. He was about to say that he wasn't going to do it, I know he was. He just didn't have the time before you all destroyed the door and knocked us to the ground. He wasn't going to do it."

I swipe at my eyes and the cop nudges a box of Kleenex toward me. I nod my thanks and grab one, blowing my nose.

"So you know each other from school?" he asks.

"No," I say. "I told you, he works at the newspaper with me." I ignore the insult that he thinks I'm still in high school.

And then I realize that by now he should know that I'm not a student at Warfield. I don't understand his obtuseness.

"And you worked on the notebook together, like a comic strip? Is that it? Just for fun, right?"

Again I correct him. The questions continue for over two hours. He misremembers or misunderstands what I say, asking the same questions over and over: What did I know of Jason's plans, of his background? Did I know he hated school? Who did we buy the guns from?

"I didn't know he had guns."

My denial brings out the first flash of temper from the cop.

"You're a liar," he spits. Something nasty flashes in his eyes, and I sit back in my chair, suddenly afraid.

The door to the room opens and another cop pops his head in.

"Frank Hale from the paper is here. Says she works for him."

The cop, reverting to that friendly-looking expression that I've grown to distrust, rises and says he'll be right back.

I wait alone in the room for about fifteen minutes, which is plenty of time to kick myself and hate myself for this new failure. I have time to wonder if I'll spend the night in jail. Time to worry that maybe I do need an attorney. But before I can request my one phone call, a different cop comes in and tells me I'm free to go.

Disoriented by the sudden release, I step out of the room into a busy hallway. Turning back, I see I was right: the mirror is two-way, and with a shiver I wonder who was standing there, watching and listening as I explained myself over and over again.

I follow the cop or administrator or whoever he is, expecting that at any minute someone will call out to stop me. Walking down the hall, I feel like a criminal, and I'm not really sure why. The man punches a code that unlocks a set of doors and suddenly we're back in the main station room, where Frank is waiting, looking completely out of place in his pale linen suit. I have never been so happy to see his Humpty Dumpty little shape. I run over and hug him.

"You've had a rough night, poor thing," he says, patting my back awkwardly.

"Thank you for coming," I say.

"Anything for my star reporter." I don't like the glee in his voice.

There are some bureaucratic steps we have to go through, and then I'm released. I don't know what Jason's been saying, but he isn't coming with us.

I walk with Frank to his boat of a Cadillac, parked crookedly, taking up two spots.

"They searched your place," he says. "That's what took so long. I've been here for a while, but the folks at the station wanted to wait and hear if they found anything. Luckily for you, your place is clean as a whistle."

"I hope Mo didn't cause a fuss when they showed up at the door," I say.

"Mo?"

"My brother's staying with me."

"There wasn't anyone in the apartment. They actually

thought they'd find some of Jason's stuff there, figured he'd hole up with you after the fact, assuming he didn't shoot himself in the head like a lot of these maniacs do. But there was nothing there but your stuff. Like I said, luckily for you."

I'm numb. Mo's gone? All his stuff? Maybe I'm not surprised; it just hurts to have it shoved in my face.

As he pulls away, bumping over a sidewalk median, Frank doesn't stop talking. "I can't believe that little snake. After all Warfield has done for him, to plan a thing like that. But thanks to you, we've got us a beaut of a scoop. I expect a piece from you on this by tomorrow. We're gonna scoop the *Tennessean*," he crows, almost running into a fire hydrant in his excitement.

We arrive at my apartment building in one piece, and I open the car door. The dome light comes on, reflecting brightly off Frank's shiny forehead.

"Thanks for vouching for me and getting me out of there, Frank," I say. "I've had a long day. I'll see you at the paper tomorrow."

"Bright and early," he says. "This story will make your career!"

He pulls away, swerving into the opposite lane before righting himself and sailing on. I stand outside for a moment, breathing in the damp night air.

There's a low cloud cover reflecting the city lights, so even though it's nighttime, the sky is a pale, evil-looking orange. There are no stars out, no visible moon. The air is still and thick, and occasional flashes of heat lightning flicker from miles away.

My heart flutters, beating quickly but inefficiently. I know better than to rail against God; it's not His fault. But the injustice of what happened burns. I was so close to helping Jason, so close to fulfilling what I was tasked with.

And Mo. I close my eyes in despair.

What about Mo?

XXVI.

ONCE I'M BACK IN THE APARTMENT, I take a minute to gather my thoughts; then I call Mo's cell phone.

"I was beginning to worry," he says in lieu of a greeting. "I thought maybe those stupid pigs arrested you too."

"They did," I say, sitting down on the couch and closing my eyes.

"Bet they felt like idiots once they realized who you were."

I ignore that, although I would say the mood at the station was one of exhilaration, the kind that comes after a job well done.

"Mo, how could you do it? How could you bring in the police? You'd promised you'd help me." *How could you toss this boy, who considered you a friend, to the wolves?*

"Miriam," he says, his voice rising. "It was the only thing to do. You didn't think you could just talk him out of it, did

253

you? He would have told you what you wanted to hear and then gone and done what he wanted to do."

Miserably, I shake my head. "That's not true," I say. "I was getting through to him. And besides, we agreed we'd convince him not to do anything. He's in jail now, do you not understand that?"

He laughs hollowly. "Miriam, he's not stupid. He knew exactly the right response to give you. I promise you he'd have brought the guns to school tomorrow. You're naïve if you think anything else. Look at it this way: If I'm right and he wasn't stopped and then he killed some students, you fail, and God smites you. If you're right, you still saved the students, Jason isn't a murderer and God doesn't have any reason to hurt you. Besides," he says in a singsong voice that pisses me off, "won't the Almighty know whether or not Jason had a change of heart?"

"I was supposed to save him. Now his life is ruined."

"Look, who did most of the talking, you or him?" he challenges. "I bet you a hundred bucks you talked and talked and he nodded and pretended to agree. What else did you think he would do?" I ignore the accuracy of that.

"You helped him get those guns, didn't you?" I accuse, refusing to let him worm away from his part in this. "Then you leaked it to the police. He didn't stand a chance, you made sure of that. You better expect a knock on your door once the police realize it's *your* handwriting."

"Don't worry about me," he says smugly. "Jason's not going to rat on me. The boy worships me. As he should."

Mo has always been a little arrogant and callous, but I

don't know who this manipulative, heartless person is. "Mo, what is wrong with you?"

"Miriam," he says slowly, as if speaking to a drunk or a young child. "You wanted to stop a school shooting. That's what I said I'd help you with, and that's what I did." I fight the persuasion in his too sincere voice. He doesn't dispute helping Jason procure the weapons. "The only way to know for sure that he wouldn't go through with it was to put him away. I wasn't planning the party alone. Jason was a willing and happy conspirator, except he would have actually pulled the trigger, the crazy fuck, and I wouldn't."

When I don't respond, I can practically hear Mo shrug. "You've had a long day," he says. "You should go to bed. After a good night's sleep, you'll see I'm right. You told me yourself even your tattooed boyfriend agreed that getting the police involved was the only way."

I sniff.

"He's not getting executed," Mo says sharply. "He'll go to juvie for a couple of years, where, frankly, he'll probably be happier than at freaking Warfield. He'll get out and go to community college, records sealed, and fulfill his 'wonderful' potential that you're so freaking obsessed with."

He's wrong, of course. But I don't have the energy to argue.

A part of me realizes this is the compromise Mo made to keep himself safe. No shooting, but at least one life irreparably ruined. I can't really muster anger. I'm too drained. So I make peace with Mo. Then I make my way to bed.

I tell myself, over and over again, that Mo meant well.

255

That this was his way of helping. Maybe that counts as much as anything else. I got him to care, to stop heartbreaking violence. Certainly my vision of Judge Bender sentencing Jason to five consecutive life sentences won't come to pass. No matter how stiff his punishment, he won't get that kind of sentence for a foiled plot. In the end, the shooting was stopped. No matter what, I have to remember to take comfort in that. Maybe having Mo love me and help me, even in a way that I didn't want—maybe that counts for something. A white mark on his soul. Maybe he'll think twice the next time the devil comes around. I don't know how to weigh the good and the bad in this case. I don't know how God will judge us.

You would think, with all this banging around in my head, that I would lose another night's sleep. You would think I'd worry about Jason spending the night in jail, or wonder where Mo went in such a hurry. But to my surprise, I soon fall into a deep, dreamless sleep.

When I open my eyes again, it's morning.

The newsroom is in an uproar. As soon as I enter, before I even boot up my computer, Frank's at my side with a gleam in his eye.

"Well, I'll be damned," he says.

I cringe at his choice of words. "You really shouldn't say that."

"I finally figured it out, you know."

"What?"

"'Sick days'?" He makes air quotes. "'Dr. Messa'?"

"Yeah?"

"You could have told me you were going undercover. We might be a small paper, but we are a newspaper and I would have supported you. No one would have known."

"You think I did this for a story?" I ask, astonished.

Frank rubs his hands in delight, ignoring me completely.

"I never thought you had it in you. You are a true journalist." I know this must be high praise in Frank's book, but to me it sounds a little hollow. "I want your feature on this as soon as possible, two thousand words minimum. We're going to spank the *Tennessean!* I'll need your piece on my desk by this afternoon. Get to work," he says; then, muttering to himself something about a special edition, he hustles off like a busy mallard duck.

With a dejected sigh, I turn to the blank screen and begin telling Jason's story. It isn't going to be what anyone wants to read, but it's the least I can do for him. Over the course of the day, several of my co-workers come over to congratulate me. But when they sense my mood, they cluck their tongues at the sad state of the world and then drift off again. Alex glares at me from across the room. I can't imagine why he's pissed off, unless he somehow thinks I've upstaged him as "star reporter," but frankly I can't spare the emotion to even feel wronged.

I write:

> Jason was not a people person. An adolescence of not fitting in had taken its toll on his soul. When I first met him, I thought he was

an obnoxious brat, and he sensed that, the same way he sensed every time that people judged him. So he gave everyone what they expected, and he sank deeper into a morass of despair.

I break the cardinal rule of journalism and use the first person. A reporter is supposed to come across as completely impartial, reporting facts, not opinions, and giving analysis without taking sides. That's ridiculous, of course: humans are incapable of completely filtering out their own impressions when they analyze facts. This time, for this story, I don't even try.

But he wasn't without merit and he wasn't lacking in gifts. Jason's talent for sketching, for capturing the essences of expressions, the nuances of posture, is remarkable for an untrained teenager. If this were a Hollywood story, then, after his years of misery, a successful artist would come across Jason's sketches and whisk him away to New York, where Jason would be accepted into a prestigious art school and be showered with accolades, fame and success. But this isn't Hollywood, and that's not how Jason's story goes.

By the end of the day, I've finished the piece. I e-mail it to Frank and then shut down my computer.

Instead, after years of junior high and high school misery, when the people who should have supported and protected him, out of misguided love, delivered him to his antagonists, Jason began to fantasize about revenge. About turning the tables on those who ignored him, mocked him, belittled him. Egged on by false friends, he sketched out how it would go: the gory shooting, the groveling preppies, the vindication of being important and mattering, if only in this horrible, terrifying way. He even procured the weapons to bring about the catastrophe he had sketched.

I leave the office before Frank has a chance to comment. Most of the coverage on Jason will skewer him. This is the one piece of kindness I can offer to him. I think of Jason's lovely eyes and the unshed tears and I know that I am probably the last person for a long time to care about either. This clearly isn't the scoop Frank was hoping for. He can either publish it or not. I'm not making any changes.

If he had gone through with his plan, then he would be a monster and deserving of all our hate, our anger, our vengeance. The difference between that monster and a fellow human deserving of our sympathy comes down to a choice. Jason didn't go through with it. And not because the police broke down his apartment door and handcuffed him as he lay pressed into the carpet. He had changed his mind before there were any repercussions. He wasn't going to bring the guns to school; he wasn't going to hurt anyone.

Jason was not an easy person to like: he lacked charm. He alienated much more easily than he beguiled. But he is being punished for a choice he did not make. How can we, a society founded on the principle of freedom, ignore free will? How can we punish evil thoughts and dark fantasies?

If we believe that each of us has a choice to do good or evil, then how can we punish someone who faced the devil's temptation but, after struggle and contemplation, rejected the choice, siding instead with his humanity? This is the essence of humanity: our ability to struggle with ourselves, to consider right and wrong and make a choice.

I cannot undo what either Jason or Mo has done. All three of us had motivations that were less than pure. All three of us are flawed, selfish and lost. Yet Jason is the one who will shoulder the brunt of the fallout. This article is my attempt, however small and insignificant, to lessen the blow.

The road to hell is paved with good intentions, the old

saying goes. And yet I find that intent does count for something. I have to believe that or everything we do here on earth is pointless.

I remember how I felt when Tabitha was hurt. Personally devastated, I could barely think straight, blinded by panic and guilt.

It's different this time.

Perhaps Raphael has taught me a bit about what all good doctors know. I tried to save someone and I didn't succeed. Yeah, it hurts. It's awful knowing the truth, knowing how Jason has been manipulated. But at the end of the day, it's me I have to answer to, me I have to live with. God watches over us and shows us the way, while the devil trips us and hopes that we fall. We can keep each other company. We can lend a helping hand. But we have to do the walking ourselves. I walked with Jason as far as I could.

But Mo is still walking nearby and the hike isn't over yet. Not yet.

I head over to Emmett's shop, where some locals are hanging out. I don't know their names, but I recognize the tattoos. I hear them mention Jason and realize that for all Frank's desire to scoop the *Tennessean*, the news is already out. Emmett looks up when the bell tinkles. He straightens from his slouch against the counter when he sees me, looking surprised but pleased. It's the first time that I realize how much I count on him to be there for me.

"You okay?" he asks, his voice low and gravelly.

Mutely I nod and walk toward him. He puts his arms

around me and the others fall silent, but I don't care that they're watching.

"You were right all along," Emmett says. With my ear pressed to his chest, his words rumble, vibrating against my skull. "But, Miriam, you can't save people who don't want to be saved."

He can't mean my brother, because he doesn't know. But it applies to Mo as much as it does to Jason, doesn't it?

"He changed his mind, you know," I say. "I talked to him and he wasn't going to do it." Which also applies to both of them.

"He said that?" Emmett asks.

I shake my head. "That's the problem. I can't testify in court that he said that, because the police barged in right as he was about to talk. But I know what he was going to say. It was obvious from the look on his face."

That's something Frank will demand to know. He'd be happy, since it's just another kind of scoop. But that devilish timing . . . the police interrupted Jason before he could say a word, and saying it now that he's been arrested won't help him. No one will believe it's genuine.

"You still did the right thing," Emmett says firmly.

"I had it under control until the police showed up and ruined everything."

"Weren't you the one who called the police?"

"No. Mo did. Even though I told him I'd be able to convince Jason, he did it anyway," I say bitterly.

Emmett doesn't say anything, which I appreciate since I

can tell that he agrees with Mo: having the police arrest Jason was a guarantee that he wouldn't hurt anyone but himself.

A part of me wonders what will happen now that I've failed again. A part of me is grieving for Jason. He's already been tried and judged, and in the town's eyes he's guilty.

Tabitha and Jason, both in the let-down-by-Miriam club. Membership is rather exclusive. I wonder if I've kept Mo off the list. Maybe I have. By a hair. On a technicality.

"Come on," Emmett says, placing a warm hand on my shoulder. "Let's go for a ride." It's his answer to all of life's curveballs. But it sounds mighty fine right now. I suck in a deep breath, hold it for a second, then blow it out, pushing away the worry and guilt.

"To the French café?" I ask, a ray of sunshine breaking through my gloom.

"*Bien sûr,*" he says with a surprisingly good French accent.

"And the scenic overlook?"

He smiles at my hopeful tone.

"We'll get some food to go and picnic up there. The fore-casters are saying this is going to be a beautiful day."

My problems, my worries, will still be here. But going with Emmett for a drive and a picnic is like pushing the pause button.

"And you're okay to leave the shop?" I ask.

He shrugs.

"It's—" he begins.

"—quiet today," I finish for him, laughing. "But what about your friends?"

The group, all shaved heads and glinting metal piercings, are milling around at the back, giving us space.

"They're leaving now. Right, guys?" He raises his voice a bit, as if they haven't been eavesdropping all along.

"Sure," they call. "No worries." They make their way out. One pats me on the back as he passes, a fatherly sort of gesture that's odd coming from one in a studded dog collar and leather pants.

"Thanks, Emmett," I say. I squeeze his hands. "You've been an amazing friend."

"Ouch," he says, smiling ruefully. "Friend, huh?"

"Well . . ." Am I flirting?? What is that tone in my voice? "What would you call it?"

He flashes a wicked smile that makes me feel warm. "I'd call it," he says, "something a bit . . ."

I wait almost breathlessly, knowing he's toying with me.

"What?" I ask when the pause has stretched beyond my tolerance. "What would you call it?"

He laughs, the sound happy and rich. Then he leans down and kisses me full on the lips.

I close my eyes at the feel of his lips on mine, but when there's nothing else, I open my eyes again to see him smiling mischievously. The friends whistle out catcalls from the door, shouting for us to get a room, obviously making fun of such a short, chaste kiss.

"I call it something more than that," he says.

"I can live with that," I say, and slip my hand into his.

We leave the shop and the still-laughing friends

congregating on the steps. The tinkling bell on the door jingles behind us as we leave.

It's another gift, this moment with Emmett. I pause to feel the sun on my face, to notice the light breeze carrying the smell of jasmine.

Job was right when he said that the Lord giveth and the Lord taketh away. But I know that He gives much more than He takes. You just have to pay attention.

Emmett drives and we leave Hamilton behind. We travel on quiet country roads with the windows down and the radio blasting golden oldies, velvet-voiced men singing "Lean on Me" and about love that fills up your senses.

I have doubts still. And questions galore. Yet I find that I have all the answers I need.

ACKNOWLEDGMENTS

Novels might be written in solitude, but they're really a team sport. I've had the literary equivalent of world-class coaches and trainers, and an Olympic-caliber cheering section, without which I never would have been able to write this, or any other book.

Erin Clarke—my fabulous editor at Knopf, who takes my words and makes them so much better. Sarah Hokanson—it's okay to judge a book by its cover as long as she designed it. Artie Bennett, Susan Goldfarb, Amy Schroeder—for crossing *t*'s and dotting *i*'s, thank you. Stephen Barbara—my terrific agent, who believes in me and in my angels.

Rabbi Danielle Upbin—a true spiritual leader, thank you for sitting down with me and decoding the mysteries of Jacob's ladder.

Prof. James F. Strange—who made time for a total stranger, thanks for an amazing, impromptu lecture on the nature of angels.

Dan Laufer—thanks for the tramp stamp heads up!

Sweetwater Farm in Tampa—who took six acres and turned them into paradise, a study of just how much is really possible when we dream.

Derek Eberhart—for Tattooing 101.

Tovar and Delaney—who make my life joyful and funny. Hiya!

Fred—my best friend, my first reader, my common sense and knot unraveler.

My mom—for teaching me how to make kidney pie aka how to deal with cancer. You are my hero.